ENDGAME TANGO

TREADWWELL SUPERNATRUAL DIRECTIVE BOOK THREE

ORLANDO A. SANCHEZ

ABOUT THE STORY

When the dance is deadly, it takes two to tango.

By absorbing the Sacred Amethyst, Regina has merged with an artifact of great power. When Cinder neutralizes the Amethyst, Regina is no longer in danger from the deadly side effects of the jewel.

There's only one slight complication.

In an effort to increase her power, Regina has removed the failsafe Cinder placed on the Sacred Amethyst, neutralizing its power.

With the amethyst unbound, Regina experiences a power shift, allowing her to ascend as a mage while taking control of Maledicta--the group of mage assassins.

Slowly, the power of the Sacred Amethyst is transforming her, awakening her darker side. With this awakening, she poses a risk to everyone—especially Sebastian and the Stray Dogs. Now, she's convinced there's only one way for her to have what her heart desires more than anything in the world —Sebastian Treadwell.

In order to have him in her life, she must remove all

distractions and obstacles. For her, there's only way to free Sebastian, she must completely destroy the Treadwell Supernatural Directive and everyone in it.

Love and hate are two sides of the same coin. Any moment, it can flip the other way. One can become the other.
-Sadhguru

"Love is blind, and lovers cannot see the pretty follies that they themselves commit."
—Shakespeare

ONE

I had finally managed to get some peace and quiet, closing the door to my office, when Rabbit's voice came over my phone.

I took a deep breath and let it out slow, gathering my thoughts and bracing myself for some fresh, new, impending apocalypse she was about to share.

"You have a visitor, Boss," she said, her voice just this side of jovial. "He insists on seeing you even without an appointment."

"I don't get visitors," I said, irritated. "Let me correct that —I don't make it a policy of accepting visitors, especially unannounced and unexpected visitors. Definitely not here at the Church. Tell them I'm out for the foreseeable future."

"He said you would say that," she said. "Instructed me to tell you that it would be in your best interests to meet with him. He said to tell you he has his eyes on you. Really felt the need to emphasize *eyes*."

I groaned inwardly.

Only one person ever had the audacity to call me by that

nickname. If he was here, my morning had just gone from relatively tranquil to cataclysmic.

"Were those his exact words?" I asked, taking a long pull from my Death Wish coffee. "Where is he now and is he alone? Did you happen to see a small, electrical lizard with him?"

"An electrical what?"

"Never mind. Trust me, you would know if his associate was here."

"His associate is a small lizard?" she asked. "Have I ever told you that you have some odd friends?"

"More than once," I said. "Were those his exact words?"

"Those were his exact words," Rabbit confirmed. "He acted like he knew you. I told him to wait in reception, but he wanted to tour the place. Said the Church has character, and that he could find you on his own. I was half-tempted to send him downstairs, but then he would be lost down there for who knows how long."

"Not long enough."

"Should I have stopped him? He looks dangerous...and homeless."

"He looks dangerous because he is," I said. "He looks homeless because...well, because street scruffiness is what passes for his style. You did the right thing. I'm sure he'll work his way to my office shortly."

"If you say so," she said. "Do you know him?"

"I do," I said, rubbing a temple to stave off the headache that was forming. "His name is Grey and he's a Night Warden."

"He looks more like a grunge," she replied. "Night Warden? They're still around? I thought they were all killed?"

"Not for lack of trying," I said. "Grey belongs to the too-old-and-crotchety-to-die club."

"Ahh, got it," she said. "What do you want me to do? I

could always have Ox escort him off the premises with extreme violence."

"No," I said with a sigh, knowing how futile that would be. Despite his appearance, Grey was one of the stronger mages I knew. Ever since his acquisition of a cursed blade, he had only grown stronger. Ox wouldn't stand much of a chance against him. "Ox doesn't deserve that kind of punishment—besides, he wouldn't succeed. Grey is much more than he appears to be. He'll find me...eventually. Thank you, Rabbit."

"If you say so," she said. "Shouldn't all the Night Wardens be retired by now? He must be old enough to be a museum relic."

"You would think they would have the sense to know when it was time to step away from the madness, but Grey never did have much of a sense of self-preservation," I said, "or any sense for that matter—he still patrols the streets."

"Wow, not bad for a senior citizen."

Grey casually opened my rune-secured door and stepped into my office as Rabbit finished her last sentence.

"Show some respect to your elders," he said, his voice gruff. "And I'm not that old."

"Whatever you say, grandpa," Rabbit snapped back. "I see he found you."

"He did," I said, looking at the door and motioning for him to fully enter my office. "I'll take it from here."

"Call me if you need anything, Boss," she said. "I'm sure we can scramble up some Ensure or warm milk and pudding for your guest. Let me know if I should send up a blanket and some pillows too. I hear when mages get to his age, they like mid-morning naps."

She laughed and hung up.

"Hilarious," Grey deadpanned, "really."

"You really should consider retiring, you know."

"I will," he said. "When I stop breathing."

He sat in one of the chairs facing my desk and gazed around the office for a few seconds in silence.

"I like this headquarters better," he continued. "Your place uptown felt too sterile. This place actually has character."

He was wearing his usual—black T-shirt, jeans, construction boots, and over it all, a worn and beaten runed-inscribed duster.

"This fashion sense of yours, senior citizen vagabond," I said, "have you ever thought of upgrading this look to respectable, productive member of society?"

He gazed at me for a few seconds.

"You mean like you?"

"I wouldn't go that far," I said. "Though, one could dare to dream."

"Do you know why I dress this way?"

"Do I want to know?"

"Because, unlike some mages or some mage groups who have high-end headquarters, the threats I deal with are on the street," he said. "I dive into the trenches, while some mages"—he looked around the office—"spend their time in fancy offices."

"Grey as spectacular as it is to see you again—and it truly is the highlight of my day," I said, gesturing and materializing another hot mug of Death Wish for him, "in fact, I'm comparing your visit to a voluntary root canal without anesthesia—I'm fairly certain you're not here to pass judgement on my lifestyle. What's going on?"

"Sebastian, you have a problem."

I sighed and pinched the bridge of my nose, as he took his mug and raised it in my direction in a show of thanks, before taking a long pull.

"Not bad," he continued. "That's why I'm here."

"My problem started the moment you walked into my

office," I said, working hard not to let anger creep into my voice. "Why are you here *exactly*, Grey?"

He placed his mug on my desk and stared hard at me. It was slightly unnerving, because I knew Grey possessed a tenant in his mind. I didn't know if it was him or his psychotic goddess looking at me.

With my luck, probably both.

"This is why you do *not* get involved with dragons," he said, pointing in my direction. "I thought you knew this. Everyone knows this. Don't *you* know this?"

I paused at his words, but maintained my composure. If he was mentioning dragons, this could be nothing good. If he felt the need to come see me in person, the odds of whatever it was being horrific had just risen stratospherically.

"I know that somewhere in that convoluted mess you call a brain, there's a point," I said, keeping my voice even. "I would truly appreciate it if you made it."

"Actually, you have two problems, Eyes," he said, raising two fingers. "Both of them need to be dealt with yesterday."

I sat behind my desk and took a long pull from my mug. It wasn't even dawn, and I knew it was going to be a long day.

He only called me Eyes when things were beyond catastrophic, and he didn't care about offending me, since he knew I absolutely abhorred that nickname.

I took another breath and kept it under control.

"What possessed me to ever give you the address to the Church?"

"Because you're a smart man," he said. "Besides, I would have found you anyway—Tiger owes me."

I rubbed my temple again.

As much as I wanted to deny it, Grey was a good friend, a valuable asset, and I was thankful he had not surrendered to darkness. Despite his questionable actions and self-professed position of being a darkmage, he was what I would consider a good person.

His methodology left much to be desired, but outside of Char, no one was more connected to the street than he was.

In fact, he was probably more connected than Char; his reach touched the pulse of the streets. Char may have been an information broker, but Grey was a Night Warden.

Those who dwelled in the shadows, who worked and lived in the darkness, knew of Char and respected her. Those same beings knew Grey and feared him. Between the two—Char and Grey—I would consider him more effective at moving in the world of shadows and getting results.

He had a particular policy of hands-on interaction that struck fear in the heart of the night. Everyone thought twice about crossing Char, because her retaliations were lethal and far-reaching. It spoke to his threat level, that no one who walked the shadows thought about crossing the Night Warden.

I took another pull from my mug and stared at Grey.

If something happened on the streets, Grey either knew about it, or knew someone who knew. If he said I had a problem, it wasn't a matter of *if*, it was a matter of *how large*.

In for a penny, in for a pound.

"How bad is it?" I asked. "I can assume monumental, since you're here gracing me with your presence."

He nodded and took another pull before answering.

"Have you spoken to Cynder?"

My blood ran cold.

"Grey...why would I need to be speaking to Cynder?"

Tiger walked silently into my office and stood in the doorway. Grey gave no indication that he had noticed her enter, but I knew him. He had probably sensed her while she was a level away.

"Shit, she didn't tell you," he said, followed by a few more curses. "Damn dragons, you can't trust them, much less get in bed with them. What the hell were you thinking? You're smarter than this. I know you're smarter than this, Eyes."

"What do you mean 'get in bed with them'?"

He pointed at my hand and the mark that pulsed softly there.

"That, Sebastian," he said. "You let Char mark you as part of her enclave?"

"Yes," I said. "There wasn't much of a choice involved."

"There's always a choice," he said, without turning. "Right, Tiger?"

"True, Night Warden," Tiger said.

"Keeping those claws sharp?"

"How do you even do that?" Tiger said. "I didn't say a word. I was barely breathing."

"I'm old and crafty," he said. "Plus, you're loud." He kept his gaze focused on me. "You're both Charkin? Are you insane? Why would you let her do that?"

I looked down at the mark that pulsed slowly, before nodding in response.

"Are you asking me as Grey, my friend, or Grey the last Night Warden of questionable repute?" I asked, my words measured and laced with danger. "The same one who unleashed an entropic dissolution in this city in a failed attempt to undo a cast, and then later on, bonded to a cursed blade which is currently the domicile of a psychotic, bloodthirsty goddess? Which is it?"

Tiger let out a small gasp and stared at me.

Had I taken it too far? Yes. He was my friend, but he did not have the right to question my choices, just as I didn't have the right to question his.

He chose to unleash an entropic dissolution to save the woman he loved. He failed and she died, and it nearly cost him his life. Accepting the cursed blade wasn't a matter convenience, I understood the circumstances and I would've done the same if it meant preserving my life. Did I feel it was wrong? Yes. However, that didn't give me the right to question his choice.

As his friend, I was able to see the situation and respect his choice, even if I disagreed vehemently with the outcome.

I needed to make that distinction clear between us, or this *conversation* would devolve into violence, and I wasn't certain either of us would emerge unscathed from *that* conflict.

Grey gave me a hard look and shook his head slowly, never removing his gaze from my face. After a few seconds, he glanced to the side and let out a long breath before turning to face me again.

"I'm asking as your friend, because if I were sitting here as a Night Warden, you wouldn't have lived long enough to finish that sentence."

We stared at each for several seconds before I nodded and gave him a curt nod.

"My apologies," I said, raising a hand in surrender. "I meant no offense, nor do I question your judgment. You did what you felt was necessary in the circumstance; I'm not one to pass judgment on your actions. I would've done the same had the—"

"No," Grey said, cutting me off. "You will not do the same. You can't. The decision I made didn't save Jade and nearly cost me everything and everyone else."

"I don't understand—"

"Promise me, Sebastian," he continued. "If you are ever faced with a choice like that, a choice where you know you can't save her, that no matter what you do, there is only one answer: that you do the right thing."

"Grey...you have my attention," I said, keeping my voice

calm, even as my intestines tied themselves into knots. I had never heard him speak this way. "What happened?

"Your lady, Regina, escaped the Eyrie."

"Holy shit," Tiger said. "What do you mean, escaped?"

"Escaped?" I asked, concerned. "I didn't realize she was being held captive."

"From where I'm sitting, there are a few things you're not realizing," he said. "I can't believe Cynder didn't say anything, but actually I'm not surprised because—dragon."

TWO

"How did she escape the Eyrie?" I asked. "From what I recall, that place has the height of security."

"That would be the second problem," Grey said. "She actually managed to thwart their security fairly easily."

"That is bad," Tiger said. "That place is a fort to get into and impossible to escape."

"And the first?" I said. "What could possibly be worse than Cynder holding her captive and her escaping a dragon's custody—and if I'm being honest, it is a little hard to accept she could break out of the Eyrie."

Grey took a pull from his mug and stared at us before releasing a short sigh. He ran his hand through his hair, and I could tell he was stalling. Whatever he was going to share would not be good.

"Just break it to us," I said. "I know it's bad."

He nodded.

"The neutralization of the Sacred Amethyst didn't take," Grey said and took another long pull from his coffee before continuing. "That would be the first problem."

"Slash me sideways," Tiger said under her breath. "How?"

"Don't know, and right now, I would think that's not the priority."

"What exactly does that mean?" I asked, perplexed. "It didn't take?"

Grey stood and reached into one of his duster's pockets. He rummaged in there for close to ten seconds before pulling out his arm, which held a small, black notebook.

The pockets of his duster were specially designed to be pocket dimensions which were larger on the inside than they were on the outside. Time and relative dimension in space, when it came to Grey's duster, didn't adhere to any known laws of physics.

It was a feature the Wordweavers, specifically Aria, had designed for his dusters. You could see why I would be concerned—what with the Wordweavers being involved around this Sacred Amethyst and Regina.

They were always up to something not exactly official or sanctioned, usually their projects ended up having potential catastrophic consequences.

"Excuse me a second," he said, turning the pages. "I had to do some research on this whole thing. Give me a moment."

Tiger smiled.

"Look at you, channeling your inner Columbo," she said, trying to get a peek at the interior of his notebook, which he prevented by shifting his body away from her. "Do you have a list of suspects in there too?"

Grey found the page he was looking for and turned to me, continuing to block Tiger's view.

"I had to do a bit of legwork to get this information," he said, glancing at Tiger. "Aria and Heka weren't exactly the most forthcoming with the details about the copy they made, or the original they were basing it on."

"Wordweavers being cagey?" Tiger said, rolling her eyes. "What a surprise. I never would've expected *that* from them."

Grey ignored her.

"The Sacred Amethyst Heka recreated was based on a real artifact, the Amethyst of Tears," Grey said, looking at his notes. "I had to go see Professor Ziller for this."

"Ziller?" I said, impressed. "You went to the Living Library for this information? You went and researched actual books, or did you locate a member of the Library for your information?"

"Books this time, thankfully," he said. "Those members of the Living Library can be a little unsettling."

"Why did you see Ziller?" I said. "Surely that information was readily available elsewhere?"

"You're not understanding what's going on here," Grey said. "That copy Heka created wasn't supposed to be a corrupted amplifier. It was supposed to just be a runic amplifier—which is dangerous on its own—but when she rearranged the runes to increase the properties, it seems to have added the corruption."

"Why not destroy it right then?" Tiger asked. "That would be the smart play. No one wants to create a deliberately corrupted amplifier, right?"

Grey gave her a look and a nod.

"You wouldn't think so, would you?" Grey continued. "Unless you were creating a weapon *designed* to be stolen."

"What?" I said, trying to understand the implications of what Grey was saying. "They wanted the sacred amethyst to be stolen?"

"Probably not at first," Grey said, holding up a hand. "I'm still fleshing out all the details, but something smells here. They had the means and the opportunity to shut this whole project down, but they didn't. Why not?"

"They left the Wordweaver who stole the gem alive," I said. "As far as I know, Amina the Wordweaver thief wasn't stripped of her abilities. That's odd in itself."

"They should've dealt with her," Tiger said. "If they weren't going to eliminate her, why not at the very least, erase her?"

"Well, Wordweavers aren't known to be cold-blooded killers, but at the very least, this is a serious breach of trust," Grey said. "I've heard of Wordweavers being erased and banned for less. As far as I know, this Amina is still at the Cloisters."

"And alive," Tiger said. "There's more there. I know it."

"Possibly, but that doesn't address the immediate situation," Grey said. "We need to focus on Regina."

"You said the neutralization didn't take," I said. "Can you explain?"

"Cynder's person, and I use the term lightly," he said as he turned a few pages in his notebook, "this Beatrix—who is a dragon by the way, did you know that?"

"Wow, Sherlock, you figured that all out on your own?" Tiger mocked, still trying to get a look at the pages of his book. "If it smells like a dragon, talks like a dragon, has the energy signature of a dragon, and threatens to rip your heart out like a dragon, chances are...it's a dragon."

"Well, in any case, Beatrix did her job well," Grey continued. "She managed an effective neutralization. She stabilized the amethyst and suspended its properties. I didn't even know that was possible with such an artifact."

"Then what happened?" I asked. "How is it no longer neutralized?"

"My best guess is that when Regina merged with the gem, it altered the failsafe somehow," Grey said. "She undid the neutralization which means she started the countdown."

"The countdown?" I asked, concerned. "What countdown?"

"Oh no," Tiger said. "The original countdown is now in place?"

Grey nodded.

He raised one finger before speaking.

"One month before the merging is irreversible." He raised another finger. "Another month before it destroys her."

"Then it explodes," Tiger said, her voice low. "We have to get it out of her. We don't know what kind of blast radius an artifact like that would have, even if it's a copy."

"I thought it was stable?" I said. "Beatrix said it would be stable. She said she stabilized it."

"It was, and she did," Grey said. "Once Regina destroyed the failsafe that maintained its neutral state, there went the stability. It is no longer stable."

A sudden thought surfaced and a realization dawned on me.

"Wait," I said, pointing at Grey. "What are *you* supposed to do? You're not just here as the bearer of horrible news."

Tiger turned to face Grey, her expression dark and her eyes dangerous. She may have despised Regina, but she knew how important Regina was to me. If she was important to me, she was important to Tiger.

No one attacked our people and lived to tell the tale, no one.

"How do you know all of this, and what *are* you supposed to do, Warden?" Tiger asked, menace seeping into her...everything. "There's no way you just happened to be investigating and stumbled onto Regina and this sacred amethyst. Someone called you."

Grey nodded.

"Who called you, Grey?"

"Is that really relevant?" Grey said, dodging the question. "What matters is that we find her and get that gem out of her before it's too late."

"I'd say it's pretty bloody relevant," I said, letting anger enter my voice. "Who called you?"

"Cynder."

"Slash me sideways," Tiger said under her breath. "That backbiting, double-crossing bi—"

"There's more at stake here," I said, cutting Tiger's rant short. "Cynder wouldn't have called you just for Regina. What aren't you telling us?"

"You are not going to like it," Grey said. "It's bad."

"Oh really?" I said, keeping my rage tightly under control. Venting it on Grey was pointless—besides, he wasn't the designated target. That honor was reserved for Cynder. I took a deep breath and calmed myself. "Are you of the opinion that there is any part of what you have just shared that I *do* like? Bloody hell, Grey, just say it."

"Initially, with the gem stabilized and neutralized, Cynder was going to use Regina—"

"Use Regina? How?"

"I'm getting to that," Grey said, holding up a hand. "You recall how I said you have two problems? Well, there's a wrinkle."

"A wrinkle?" Tiger asked. "Your wrinkles are beginning to be full-blown creases of disaster."

"You shared the first," I said. "What is the second?"

"Regina is the new leader of Maledicta."

THREE

"What the fu—?"

"My expression exactly," Grey said, cutting Tiger off. "Regina isn't known for wetwork—she's not an assassin. Hell of a thief—and willing to carve your heart out of your chest if you get in her way, but she's not an assassin."

"I'm familiar with the latter aspect of her disposition," I said, rubbing the spot where long ago Regina had decided I needed some alterations from her blades. "Why in charge of Maledicta?"

"I know they needed new leadership after Calum," Tiger said. "I would have never picked Regina for the job. She's not the plays-well-with-others type...unless—?"

"She was going to fulfill contracts *and* liquidate assets," Grey said. "The target would no longer need them, and Cynder would allow Maledicta to conduct business under her watchful eye. Win-win for everyone."

"Cynder gets the contracts done and Regina gets the spoils," Tiger said. "I can see that."

"She was going to exploit Maledicta, with Regina as the

new head," I said. "It's warped, ruthless, deadly, and efficient. Just the way a dragon would think."

"That was most likely the plan while the amethyst was stable," Grey said. "Now, plans have changed."

"It's no longer stable," I said, "which means—"

"Regina is now a perceived threat," Grey said. "One Cynder needs to neutralize."

"That's why she called you," Tiger said, looking at Grey. "Why you?"

"First, Dragons and I do not get along," Grey said. "Never have and never will."

"Yet here you are, working for them," Tiger shot back. "How did that happen?"

"*With* not *for*," Grey corrected. "There is a difference."

"Really? Because from where I'm standing, the end result is the same—Regina dies," Tiger said. "Why don't you make it make sense, Warden?"

"I'm listening," I said. "Why did Cynder let you take this job?"

"She owes me a blood claim," Grey said. "I called it in."

He let the words hang in the air between us.

"You have a blood claim with Cynder?" Tiger asked. "But you hate dragons."

"My dislike of dragons doesn't preclude my dealing with them when necessary," he said. "Cynder had opened this contract to some nasty individuals. Once I made the blood claim—"

"She was obligated to honor your request," I said. "That was a powerful bargaining token. Why use it for this?"

"I've been in your position," he said. "My lack of options made me act irrationally. I lost Jade and some good friends. It cost me my standing in the Wardens, and it nearly cost me my life—I could make the argument that it did cost me my life...considering the outcome. I didn't want you to go through the same thing."

"Still, I can't believe Cynder honored a blood claim," Tiger said. "She only answers to Char, and it seems she does that reluctantly."

"Dragons don't do authority well," he said. "A blood claim is different—even dragons adhere to the code. If it's not respected or honored, it means you can't be trusted. This is no light matter: once invoked, you're bound to it."

"Again, not seeing the motivation for a dragon like Cynder," Tiger said. "She is the queen of her domain and barely follows instructions from Char."

"I'm not Char," Grey said, and his voice held the promise of pain and death. "In this world, traditions and respect are paramount. We're surrounded by murderers and thieves, and those are the ones we tolerate. Without a code of conduct, chaos reigns. Even Cynder understands the wisdom of order, especially in our world."

"And right now, Regina represents chaos," I said. "If she devolves and usurps Maledicta, it can start a war. The streets will become a warzone."

"Can start?" he said, shaking his head. "No, that war has already started."

"What are you saying?" I asked. "What has Regina done?"

"She may not be an assassin, but she certainly knows how to operate like one," Grey said. "Maledicta has been dispatched to the streets. They're striking at targets of opportunity."

"Why?" Tiger asked. "They only operate when they have a contract. Isn't that the way they move?"

"It used to be," Grey said. "But the amethyst is changing her. She's gone from eliminating designated targets to undermining confidence in Cynder and her Wyverns."

"Shit," Tiger said. "That's suicide."

"I don't think Regina cares," Grey said. "In fact, I think that's the entire point. She wants to destroy Cynder and the Wyverns, along with some other groups, from what I understand."

"Other groups?" I asked. "Tell me she's not going after the Councils."

"Not yet," Grey said before taking another pull of his coffee. "Word on the street is that she is going to try and bury Cynder, her Wyverns, and one other group, at least for now."

"Who?" Tiger asked. "Maledicta has numbers but not that many—she can't go after any of the larger groups. Cynder and the Nine are going to keep Maledicta busy enough. She wants to go after someone else?"

"You," Grey said, his voice serious. "She's coming after all of you."

"All of us?" Tiger asked.

"The other reason I took this contract is because Maledicta has a KOS on the Stray Dogs," Grey said. "Regina wants *all* of you gone—except *one* of course."

"Of course," Tiger said, glancing at me. "Looks like your number one fan wants you all to herself."

Grey nodded.

"If I were you," Grey said, glancing around the office, "I'd alert your entire team to operate at the highest threat level possible. She may not be fully corrupted, but that sacred amethyst is messing with her mind. There's a good chance she's—"

Grey never finished his sentence. The runic explosion that tore through the side of the Church drowned him out.

FOUR

For a split-second, the earth went absolutely still.

A pause of everything enveloped the space, as if the universe were holding its breath in anticipation of the devastating fury that was about to be unleashed.

Then, a second later, Tiger leapt in front of Grey and me, gesturing as she moved. She threw up a wall of energy as another deafening explosion ripped through the side of the Church, gouging out a massive hole, sweeping us up in a fiery explosion and snatching us out of my office.

We spilled out on the street below to a chorus of car alarms and shattered glass. Tiger got to her feet and brushed herself off as she took in the scene.

"That could have gone sideways," she said. "Not to sound paranoid, but it's almost like your office was targeted."

"It's not paranoia when your office *is* being blown up," Grey said, adjusting his duster. "Did you redirect most of the blast?"

"Suppressed most of it...or we would be standing in the middle of a morgue out here," Tiger said, looking at me. "Any guesses who would be behind this?"

"Some," I said, "I'd rather not surmise just yet, since we only have an explosion to go on."

"I didn't realize the Directive was this popular," Grey said, looking around. "You've made some angry enemies."

People were running and screaming down the street. Several cars had collided with each other. A few had rammed parked cars, and I saw some trucks stranded on the sidewalk, their drivers unconscious.

"Tiger, we better get some first responders out here immediately," I said, taking in the scene around us. "Excellent work with that shield."

She nodded, her expression grim.

"Watch out for Maledicta," she said, letting her gaze scan the street. "Be right back, going to make some calls, get EMTes on site too. If you see your woman, do not engage her. If she did this, she's unstable."

I moved my aching body.

I was thankful for Tiger deflecting and suppressing the blast, but our landing had been rough. Still, it could have been worse, much worse.

"When *has* she been stable exactly?"

"True," she said, examining the damage, "this is more unstable than usual. She's dangerous, Seb—"

"She's always—"

"You know what I mean," she snapped. "She'll kill you and say she's helping you make up your mind as she buries the blade in your midsection. Do not engage her."

"That's the plan—non-engagement."

"I'm serious, Seb," she said, pointing at the Church. "That could've easily been us."

She took off at speed as she ran back inside the Church to alert the proper authorities.

"Bloody hell," I said, taking note of the damage, as Grey walked up beside me. "Maledicta?"

"Yes. It's a diversion," he said, looking up and pointing. "Look."

I looked up and saw the figures running across the rooftops. They moved with grace and power—living shadows with no discernible features aside from being clothed all in black and wearing short swords.

Maledicta.

Their faces and bodies were completely covered in black, leaving only their eyes visible. The clothing they wore seemed to absorb the light as they moved above us.

"Tiger has a point though," Grey said. "If Regina is behind this"—he took in the damage to the Church and the surrounding area—"she's further gone than I thought."

"You think this is a result of the amethyst?" I asked. "The damage is extensive, but it seems to be centered around the Church—and my office, specifically. Almost as if it's a message."

Grey turned to stare at me for a few seconds.

"Are you saying she's twisted enough to do this *intentionally?*" he asked, looking at the site of the explosion. "Just to get your attention?"

"She's done worse—I have the scars to prove it," I said. "You don't know Regina very well, do you?"

"I don't, but if you say she's capable of this without the amethyst's influence, I don't want to see what she's capable of when it starts to affect her mind," he said, his voice grim. "If it wasn't for Tiger, people would have died here today."

"I'm aware," I said, looking up to the rooftops at the figures racing away from the scene of the explosion. "We should see if we can apprehend one of them. Maybe ask them if they'd like to share the plan."

"I doubt they'll want to have a chat with us," Grey said with a dark smile as his gaze followed their movement. "But I can be persuasive when I need to be."

"We need one alive, Grey," I said. "It won't benefit us if you apprehend one and he can't speak because you broke him."

"What do you take me for? Some kind of monster?"

"Grey—and I say this in the most flattering way possible—there are literal monsters on the streets that fear the last Night Warden," I said. "To such an extent that they are willing to divulge information detrimental to their health to avoid running into you."

"You know, Sebastian, you really know how to lift a person's spirits," he said with a wicked smile. "That warms my arctic heart."

"I wasn't aware you still possessed one," I answered. "Detain one, alive please. I'll coordinate with the EMTes when they arrive."

"Good idea. Let me see if I can find out where they're going," Grey said. "Watch yourself, there may be some of them close by. Maintain your defenses and your situational awareness."

"Will do," I said as he moved fast, stepping into a short alley near the Church and disappearing. I sensed no expenditure of energy as he vanished from sight. "*That* is a neat trick. I wonder if he could show me—"

The short, red dagger focused my thoughts on the bright blossom of pain that materialized in my arm the next moment.

Tiger's words rushed back to me in a split-second: *If you see your woman, do not engage her.* It would seem that plan of non-engagement was heavily dependent on my seeing her first.

If I had any doubt as to the creator of my pain, it was dispelled the next moment as I saw Regina standing across the street, about twenty feet away.

She smiled and waved when I looked at her.

She wore the same clothing as the rest of Maledicta, except one of her sleeves was red. Aside from that one detail, everything else she wore was black and made of the same light-absorbing material I had seen earlier.

Despite the agony in my bicep, my heart skipped a beat and my breath caught in my chest when I saw her.

"I must be truly mental," I muttered under my breath. "She just buried a blade in your arm, Sebastian, and you're looking at her like some lovesick teenager."

Her deep red hair was pulled back and actually matched the sleeve of her garment. She always did have an eye for detail. Her eyes, which were fixed on me, flared with a wave of violet energy as she formed another dagger, allowing it to float above the palm of her hand.

As a blademaster, she had a neverending supply of blades to dispatch in my direction. Thankfully—I knew from my personal experience—the red blades she used were non-poisonous.

She wasn't alone.

Behind her stood a mountain posing as a human. He wore the same black clothing all of Maledicta seemed to favor, except he was on the extreme large side, reminding me of Ox dressed as an assassin, and standing there still as a statue and silent as death.

His dark, flat eyes focused on me, as I bled on the street.

"I thought he would never leave. Hello, Sebastian," she said, her voice surprisingly clear over the chaos around us. She kept her gaze locked on me. "I suppose I have you to thank for saving my life?"

I glanced down at the blade protruding from my arm.

"This is certainly an unconventional method of displaying gratitude," I said. "You do realize you could have just called me. There was no need to obliterate the Church to get my attention."

"True," she said, glancing at the large hole in the side of the Church. "But this was more fun and attention-getting."

I glanced at the damage to the Church.

"You definitely captured my undivided attention," I said. "Ursula is not going to be pleased. If I'm not mistaken, this property is landmarked."

"That Bear is full of herself," she said with disgust, glancing at the damage. "This will give her something to do. Plus, I needed to make sure you knew it was me."

"This certainly has your touch all over it," I said. "I don't have many people sending me explosive greetings these days."

"It looks like your new headquarters can use some renovating—you're welcome," she said. "I do like the choice, however, a church? Really, love? That's so unlike you. How gothically chic."

She laughed and then grew serious.

In the back of her eyes, the madness danced as she looked at me.

I realized I was in real danger.

Not that blowing a hole in our headquarters to get my attention left any doubt to Regina's threat level, but the madness that looked back at me drove it home.

She was indeed more unstable than usual.

I took a deep breath and opted for changing the subject to something potentially less lethal that didn't revolve around exploding my home and headquarters.

"I see you're making new friends," I said, shifting my glance to the large human wall behind her. "Who's this?"

"Oh, apologies," she said, glancing at the giant behind her. "Where *are* my manners? This is my second, Mura."

"Your second?" I asked. "Second in what? Demolitionists? What does he do, besides blot out the sun?"

"I have missed your wit," she said. "He worked for Calum, up until the moment where Calum betrayed and discarded him like trash. After my liberation, I offered him a better proposition—he could live and lead Maledicta with me, or die. He chose life."

"Wise choice, it seems."

"He's quite skilled at what he does," she said. "I'd even say he's gifted."

"What exactly is it that he does?" I asked. "Besides take up large amounts of space."

She smiled.

"He kills," she said, still smiling. "He's exceptionally gifted in the art of ending life."

"The art?"

"In Maledicta, the act of taking a life has been elevated to an art form," she explained. "Mura is one of the most accomplished artists in Maledicta."

"I was under the impression they were just assassins."

Her expression darkened, and Mura's eyes narrowed, growing flinty in their gaze.

"They are not *just* assassins," she said. "They are artists."

"That kill people," I clarified. "Why did you need liberating? What happened?"

"I liberated myself," she said. "Cynder wanted me to be her pet. I serve no creature, especially not a dragon. She and I disagreed. I destroyed the failsafes and activated the Sacred Amethyst. Taking its power for myself."

"You destroyed the failsafes," I said, staring at her. "The failsafes that were put in place to keep you from exploding in a few months?"

"Lies," she snapped. "Lies to keep me under her thumb, to keep me controlled, to keep Maledicta in her fist. Lies that I shattered."

I took a breath and sighed.

"How does Cynder benefit from lying to you?" I asked,

trying to reason with her. "She is one of the reasons you're still among the living."

"Wrong," she said, shaking her head slightly. "I hear it was someone else."

"You heard wrong," I said. "Cynder was—"

"I heard...*you* are the reason Beatrix placed the Sacred Amethyst in me," she said, cutting me off. "Cynder says that you pled for my life. That it was your decision that saved me. Is this true?"

For the briefest of seconds, I considered lying, but it would serve no purpose. Once Regina had an idea in her head, right or wrong, it became her reality. If she was under the impression that I was responsible for her being saved, nothing I could say would change that.

"Yes," I said after a pause, "but I'm beginning to think it may have been an error in judgment."

"What makes you say that?" she asked, tapping the blade that floated above her hand. "I thought you would be happy to see me?"

"I was when you facilitated my exit from the vortex—"

"That was impressive, don't you think?"

"I do," I said. "Your maneuver in the garage wasn't exactly endearing. You planned on leaving us there to die."

"I wasn't going to let Calum keep the amethyst," she said. "He was too unhinged to be allowed access to real power."

"So you double-crossed him?"

"Yes," she said. "You know artifacts are my weakness, love. If it's any consolation, I really hated leaving you behind."

"I'm sure you did," I said. "That's why Tiger brought you back...alive."

"Do you regret not letting her kill me?"

I glanced down at my arm, the blade buried in my bicep, and the blood pooling on the ground beneath me.

"Oh, the blade protruding from my arm is definitely making me reconsider some of my past life choices."

"That's just a scratch," she said, waving my words away. "I could have buried it in your chest. Would you have preferred that?"

"I seem to recall we tried that, I didn't enjoy last time," I said. "I haven't acquired a taste for impalement since then."

"Pity," she said, running her tongue across her lips. "A little pain can be a *good* thing."

"We seem to have different definitions of the word —*good*," I said, maintaining my calm. "In any case, I prefer my body to be blade-free, thank you."

She smiled.

A soft caress of cold fear gripped my spine.

"You were always so intelligent, Sebastian," she said, flexing one of her hands. Black and red energy arced between her fingers. I noticed her energy signature was considerably stronger. "I'm stronger now too. Do I have you to thank for that as well?"

As she spoke, the dagger hovering over her hand twisted and turned with her words.

"I may have had a hand in that as well," I said as she raised an eyebrow in my direction. "Think nothing of it. Consider it a gift."

She nodded as she looked down at the blade in her hand for a moment and then turned her gaze back to me.

"Maledicta...is now mine," she said, tapping the hilt of the red blade over her hand. "They serve me now...only me. I am the Shadow Queen."

"This isn't you, Regina," I said. "You are a world-class thief, yes, but assassin? This isn't you."

"You don't *know* me," she said, her voice soft. "Not any longer. You think you do, but truly, deep down, you don't know who I am in the darkness."

"I know this isn't you," I said. "I know you're no assassin."

"Are you saying I'm not *capable* of killing?" she asked, her words hard as she stared at me. "You think I *can't* kill?"

"I have no doubt about your capacity to take life," I said. "But running an assassin organization? Even one as accomplished as Maledicta—is not you. You prefer an unfettered life. You left the Treadwell Supernatural Directive, you left *me*, for that very reason. You didn't want to be tied down or responsible for others."

She looked off to the side before answering.

"That was before, but now, Maledicta presents me with new opportunities," she said. "Opportunities I could never have with you or the Directive."

"I strongly suggest against this course of action."

"That almost sounds like a warning, my love," she said. "Are you threatening me?"

"You know me, Regina," I said. "I don't threaten…I promise. If you walk this path, it will end in death. You don't want to do this."

"Oh, but I do."

"You don't understand the risk of the amethyst," I said. "It will kill you. We can stop this before it's too late."

She smiled again and shook her head.

"It's surprising how quickly they welcomed me," she said, glancing up at the rooftops and the silhouettes of the few members of Maledicta I could see. "Cynder didn't treat their last leader too well."

"Do you think she's going to treat you any better?" I asked. "You openly rebel against her. She's a dragon. They don't take that sort of thing well."

"I do," she said and smiled again, chilling my blood. "Calum was a fool. He had nowhere near my level of power. I'm as strong as Cynder—stronger even."

"Calum thought so too," I said. "He was mistaken. Going to war against Cynder and her Nine is certain death."

"For her," she said. "Cynder can't stop me. No one can."

I shook my head slowly.

"This is madness," I said. "It's not too late to stop. Let me help you."

"I'll be coming for you, my love."

"I'd rather you didn't," I said. "Not if it means you leaving death and destruction in your wake."

Her expression darkened at my words, and I feared I may have miscalculated just how deranged she may have become.

"I understand your reluctance, but consider this," she said, waving an arm around. "I did all this just to say hello and get your attention. Imagine what I would do if you refuse my invitation…I *am* coming for you. And when I do, you will leave everyone and everything behind and come with me. There is no other option. Not if you want them to remain alive."

"I see that now, my apologies," I said. "I'm afraid I'm going to have to decline your offer and end this fantasy of yours."

"You're more than welcome to try, but you and your Directive are not strong enough," she answered. "Search my energy signature and know I speak the truth."

She unleashed her full energy signature and overwhelmed me with her power. The sacred amethyst had done what it was designed to do; it had amplified her power significantly.

I took a moment to curse Heka and her tinkering for inventing something like the amethyst and allowing it to be used in this way.

"I see I was mistaken," I said, keeping my voice even. "You're much stronger than I anticipated. Too strong for me or anyone in the Directive."

She narrowed her eyes at me and smiled one more time.

"Now you're speaking like the man I love," she said. "See? That wasn't so hard was it?"

"Not at all," I said. "In fact, why don't you come into the Church? You must be exhausted from all this destruction and exploding. You could sit, have a cup of tea, and rest a bit."

"Nice try," she said, shaking her head. "But I said *I'm* coming for *you*, not the other way around. Still, the invitation was nice. Just to let you know there's no hard feelings, I'll leave you with a memento of our little moment here."

Bloody hell. Her mementos were always of the painful sort.

"That's not really—"

The blade that had been hovering over her hand, buried itself in my leg. I fell back and landed against a car parked on the street. Regina looked up into the air, narrowed her eyes and gave Mura a nod. He crouched down and jumped, attached himself to the wall about twenty feet up and scaled the building silently.

In seconds, he reached the roof and was gone.

It was both an impressive and fearsome display of power, stealth and agility for someone so large. He would be difficult to deal with in the future.

"Your second-in-command bitch is coming back," she said, glancing past me and looking into the Church. "It was wonderful catching up. We will talk again soon."

"No need to rush off on my acc—"

She gestured, forming a teleportation circle just as Tiger stepped out into the street. The next moment, Regina disappeared in a cloud of red and black energy. The circle pulsed with latent energy for a few seconds, before it too disappeared from sight.

"Seb, what the hell!" Tiger yelled when she saw the blades in me. "I leave you alone for a few minutes and you volunteer for designated pincushion?"

"Do you...do you really think I wanted these blades in me?"

"Did she use poison?" Tiger asked when she got close. "How much damage am I doing if I remove them from you?"

"No...no poison this time," I said and felt myself get lightheaded. I had lost a considerable amount of blood. The blade in my leg had missed all of the important parts, but it still posed a risk. "Take them out. I don't possess your healing ability, but I'll cast some healing—at least until we get someone more qualified."

She slowly removed the blades.

"I can't believe you," she said. "I wasn't gone ten minutes."

"For the record," I said, "there was no volunteering involved."

Those were the last words I spoke before the ground tilted sideways and reached up to tap me lightly in the forehead.

FIVE

I regained consciousness in the Church infirmary.

Outside, I heard the sirens of the EMTes leave the scene of the explosion.

"Any casualties?"

"No deaths, plenty of injured though, and major property damage," Tiger said. "Some vehicles were totaled from the explosion, and it turns out the Church is landmarked. Replacing the damaged stone is going to be a challenge."

"Has DAMNED been contacted?" I asked. "She'll want to know—especially for a landmarked property."

"Ursula shared some choice words when I told her and suggested we relocate to a less valuable headquarters if we were going to have explosive renovations in the future."

"She's all compassion," I said. "Did she inquire if anyone was hurt?"

"She had a direct line to the EMTes," Tiger said. "She knew the extent of the damage, both human and property. She was not pleased."

"I can imagine."

"No, no you can't," she said. "She also wanted to know if this *destroying the city* thing ran in the family."

"I don't follow."

"Between you and your cousin, his associate, and the hellhound, Ursula is thinking of forming a special task force just to keep track of all of you."

"First of all, *I* didn't cause this destruction," I started. "That was—"

"Save it, she wasn't hearing it," Tiger said, raising a hand. "Expect an extra spicy conversation with her when it comes to the Church repairs. You've been warned."

I nodded and looked down at my body. Both my wounds had been dressed and bandaged.

"By the way, excellent work on my wounds," I said, admiring the dressings. "Have you been practicing?"

"No," Tiger said. "I excel at *creating* wounds, not dressing them. You're looking at someone else's handiwork."

"Whose?"

"Who else?"

"Tell me you didn't call Roxanne," I said with a groan. "She'll make this into a *thing* and probably tell Tristan, which means it will get back to my Uncle Dexter. And then, he'll feel the need to have a 'talk'."

"I know how much you love those talks with your Uncle."

"You didn't."

"As much as I enjoy torturing you, I figured you've had enough pain for one day," she said with a smile. "No, I called Ivory."

"Ivory?" I said, incredulous. "She left her Tower and came here? I don't see her security. She came here alone?"

"This is Ivory...she never leaves the Tower without her security," she said. "She has her creatures outside. Actually, now that I think about it, I don't think I've *ever* seen her leave the Tower."

"She doesn't—not if she can help it."

"Yes, surprised me too," she said. "She must really like you. Imagine that."

"She's usually overwhelmed with work," I said, admiring the dressing with fresh eyes. "For her to leave the Tower...I'm flattered."

"I think you are the only person she would leave her Tower for on such short notice," Tiger said. "Now, don't move, or she's going to scream at me again, and I am *not* in the mood. She's on her way back."

"Way back?"

"She needed a few things made and stepped out to go see Goat," she said. "Said he was the best person for the project."

"Scream at you?" I asked, confused. "Why did she scream at you?"

Tiger cocked her head to one side and gave me a 'Really?' look.

"Apparently, it is *my* responsibility to keep you from being perforated by *your* psycho woman," she replied. "I am not supposed to let you be target practice for Regina's blades."

I smiled at the thought of Ivory chastising Tiger. I looked down at my wounds and winced as I adjusted my leg. The bandage around my thigh was a little tight for comfort.

"It's not funny," Tiger said. "I do not appreciate being screamed at. I've hurt people for giving me the wrong look. Raising your voice at me is a guaranteed recipe for pain."

"Well...she does have a point."

"You want to think carefully before finishing that train of thought," she warned. "It looks to me like it's headed for a derailment caused by my fists."

"You are my second—"

"Second, not babysitter or bodyguard," she said, cutting me off. "You are the Director of the Stray Dogs, and we both know you are more than capable of taking care of yourself... even against Regina."

"This is true," I agreed. "You try taking Ivory on, and she'll make sparring with Char feel like fun. I don't think you want to go there with her."

"I don't, but you need to have some words with her," she said, her voice serious. "It's not happening again...not without consequences."

"I'll make sure to speak with her."

"See that you do," she said and headed for the door. "I'll be back when she's done with you."

She stepped out of the room.

There were few beings on this plane that would risk raising their voice, much less scream at Tiger. In fact, I could probably count them on one hand.

Ivory was one of those few people.

I was alone in the room—at least for the moment. I lay my head back and closed my eyes, letting out a deep breath in the relative peace and quiet.

I sensed the presence before I saw it enter.

It wasn't a person at all, but an eight foot security guard covered in armor from head to toe. Strapped to its back was a large, lethal-looking blade to complement the assortment of blades that rested in sheaths along its legs.

A Rakshasa.

These were Ivory's personal security guards. Formidable, lethal, cunning, and highly intelligent. The golden armor it wore gleamed in the light as it took its position on the far wall.

If I knew Ivory, she had at least two Rakshasi with her. She never left the Tower without her personal guards. Usually, one was enough of a deterrent against any threat she would encounter. That, and the fact that she was an ancient ifrit with staggering power that boggled the imagination prevented any attacks.

Behind the Rakshasa, I sensed her presence.

She came into my field of vision, wearing her deep indigo set of rune-covered scrubs and matching scrub cap, along with an expression somewhere between concerned and angry.

Now I knew why the infirmary was empty.

I remained silent and gazed at her as she approached my bed. Ivory wasn't very tall physically, but she was similar to Tiger in that she emanated a presence. In Tiger's case, it was a presence of imminent and agonizing pain.

With Ivory, it was something deeper.

It was the realization that her age was most likely measured in eons. She radiated a certain weight of age. It was akin to standing next to an ancient mountain. Awe and wonder mixed with the very real potential of mind-shattering power being unleashed at you almost as an afterthought.

It was a sobering and grounding experience.

The Rakshasa stepped in and kept the door open.

SIX

Ivory stepped fully into the room.

Her eyes fluctuated between their normal pitch-black with flecks of gold to bright red flames. Her eyes were disturbing to look at under normal circumstances—the intermittent flames only made everyone nervous.

I don't think it was a conscious reaction. Whenever Ivory was upset or angry, her eyes would react this way. You could imagine that not many people went out of their way to anger her.

"Sebastian," she said, her soft voice filling the room. "Was this a poor attempt at catching blades, or have you suddenly decided to become someone's target?"

"Regina is in town," I said with a slight groan as she tightened the bandage around my thigh. "We were having a *conversation*. Does it really need to be that tight? I thought the idea was to let my blood circulate?"

She raised an eyebrow and remained silent while she worked on my bandages.

"I see," she said. "That woman—and I use the term loosely—is hazardous to your health. If memory serves, I'm the medical professional here. Yes, the bandages need to be *that tight*."

"Thank you for coming," I said with a nod. "We could have gone to the Tower. You didn't have to come all this way."

She gave me a withering glare.

"You *could* have come to the Tower, if you intended to deliver your body for an autopsy," she said. "You lost much blood. Usually, when someone suffers a stab wound, they don't take that moment to engage in *conversation*. Once the bleeding starts, it's prudent to seek medical attention."

"I needed to make sure the area was secure," I said. "That meant making sure she was gone."

"Ten more minutes and you would have been," Ivory said, shaking her head. "You are not Tiger. I strongly advise you against catching blades with your body."

"Is that your professional advice?"

She placed a hand on my shoulder and gazed into my eyes. I had never been put off by her eyes, but I had experienced some bizarre events in my life.

It was one of the reasons she and I got along so well. Nothing about her disturbed me. We were friends. For an ifrit like Ivory, having friends was a rare thing.

"I'm telling you this as your friend *and* as a medical professional," she said, gripping my arm—hard enough for me to notice. "Stop stepping into life-ending situations. One of these days, it will be the last step you take."

"I may have been the catalyst," I said. "Blowing a hole in the Church was unwarranted and excessive. There was no reason for her to react—"

"Bull," she said. "Somewhere along the chain of events that led you to this bed, you had an active hand in it. I know if I go back far enough, I will find you there, causing this situation."

I looked away.

She wasn't wrong, but it still wasn't my fault.

Except that on some level, it was. Not that I would admit it...out loud.

"I thought so," she continued. "Now, what are you going to do about Regina?"

I looked to the door and saw it had been closed with her security standing directly in front of it. I was certain that the other guard was standing immediately outside of the door, preventing any visitors from approaching my room.

"Am I being detained?" I asked with a half-smile and pointed at my leg. "I'm not exactly a flight risk."

"It's not for you."

"Is the security necessary?" I asked. "Are we expecting another attack? We're inside the Church."

"Which is where the last attack occurred."

"Touché."

"No, the security is here because I don't leave the Tower without it, and your Directive is nosy," she said. "My guards are quite effective at deterring eavesdropping."

I glanced at the Rakshasa by the door.

"I would imagine," I said. "Before we start on that topic, I need to discuss something with you."

"Yes," Ivory said, pulling up a chair and sitting beside my bed. "What do you wish to share?"

"You raised your voice at Tiger?"

She looked away and then turned back to stare hard into my eyes. In her eyes, I saw endless stars extending into the infinite, before she blinked and they reverted back to her usual solid black with gold flecks.

"Sebastian," she said with a small sigh, "you do realize I am *old*. Probably older than any entity you know, with the exception of Azrael masquerading as a deli owner—he must truly be bored."

"I do," I said. "I know you've forgotten more about

humanity than I will learn in this lifetime, but Tiger is my second. If you yell at her and then she overreacts because of it—and face it, this is Tiger, it's totally possible—you may do something irrevocable, like blast her to atoms. Could you heal her from being atomized?"

"Unlikely."

"Then you acknowledge the possibility of your disintegrating her exists?"

"This is Tiger we are discussing," she said after a pause. "There is always that possibility, true."

"I'd like to keep Tiger among the living," I said, measuring my words carefully. "Could you be *more* patient with her? It's not her fault I ended up stabbed."

"Twice," Ivory said with an edge to her voice. "Like you said, she is your *second*. Do you realize how severe the consequences would have been if during my youth a second allowed these kinds of injuries without being on a deathbed themselves?"

"We are not in your time," I said gently. "I dare say the requirements were stricter in your time."

"A second's responsibility is to keep her first safe. Before anything, Tiger is a warrior and she understands this. She walks the path of bushido."

"She is not samurai," I said. Ivory and I had had this conversation in the past. "Yes, she is a warrior, but I cannot force her to adhere to a code that is not—"

"Loyalty, family, courage, honor, self-discipline, selflessness, and sacrifice," Ivory said, cutting me off. "Does she not uphold the tenets of these qualities?"

"Well, yes."

"This is before bushido and samurai," she said. "I use that term to help *your* understanding, but the warrior way needs no title or name, it just is. It transcends culture, labels, and time."

"Is that why you raised your voice at her?"

"I raised my voice because she knows Regina is a weakness for you," Ivory said, raising a hand to prevent me from interrupting. "She left you alone and exposed, knowing you were vulnerable."

"I'm not a child," I said, mildly offended. "I can defend myself."

She gave me another long stare before glancing at my wounded leg and arm. Her silence in that moment spoke volumes.

"These wounds...is that a new method of defense?" she asked. "Where you allow the weapons to cut you to distract the attacker?"

"The first one caught me by surprise."

"You were distracted?" she asked. "On an active battlefield?"

"Preoccupied," I deflected. "People were hurt and there was much damage on the scene and to the Church."

"Preoccupied enough that I needed to dress two wounds this day," she answered, raising two fingers. "The one in your arm was serious. This is why I raised my voice, but—as you say, I am the elder here—I will take her youth and brashness into consideration in our future dealings. I will not blast her to atoms."

"Promise?"

"Sebastian, you realize I have blasted others to nothing for less?" she said. "The aegis of friendship will only protect you so far."

"Your word," I said. "I need your word, because I know Tiger and I know you, but mostly I know Tiger."

She sighed, looked away, and then nodded before turning her gaze to me once more.

"I give you my word. I will not blast Tiger to atoms as a result of her actions or words directed at me," she said.

"However, that does not preclude an ample dose of pain, enough to make her wish she were dead."

She smiled at that last sentence. As expected, I knew there would be some loophole or condition in her agreeing not to atomize Tiger.

She was an ifrit after all.

"Thank you," I said, relieved. "She can benefit from your wisdom."

Ivory laughed.

"Now you're laying it on thick," she said. "Tiger is many things; teachable is not one of them, at least not without copious amounts of pain."

"True," I said. "You said you wanted to deter eavesdropping? Is that why your Rakshasi are guarding the door?"

She glanced at the large security guard blocking the entire door.

"Yes. We need to discuss some hard truths, and I don't need you distracted by Tiger or the Night Warden."

I knew what she was talking about, even if I didn't want to voice it in the moment. Dodging the subject would help no one. I took a deep breath and let it out slow.

"Can you help Regina?" I asked. "Can you save her or reverse the effect of the amethyst? Or is it too late?"

"That depends," Ivory said, looking off to the side again. "I need to see how far gone she is. My power is considerable, but I'm not omnipotent. If the corruption of the amethyst is too advanced, the options are limited."

"Worst case scenario?"

"If the corruption is too pronounced, the woman you know will cease to exist," she said softly. "There won't be anyone you remember to save. From my understanding, she will slip into madness. You won't be able to save her, and more importantly, she won't want to be saved. She will have succumbed to the darkness."

"How will the corruption present itself? Do you know?"

"I do and so do you," she said, pointing at my bandages. "Those wounds will be love taps compared to what she will do to those who stand against her."

"Bloody hell," I said, rubbing my face. "She possesses considerable skill, being a blademaster. This will be a bloody mess."

"That's *exactly* what it will be," Ivory said. "Pain, blood, and death. She will transform into a nightmare approaching Archmage level of power."

"Approaching?"

"She will not be a true Archmage," Ivory said. "The amethyst she is merged to is not a true artifact, but a construct, which explains the corruption."

"Does the Amethyst of Tears exist?"

"Yes, but it is not accessible from this plane," she said. "The Wordweaver who created this copy, was tampering with things, with power, beyond her understanding. If Regina undergoes a complete transformation with this gem, she will leave you only one option at the end."

"I would have to end her, wouldn't I?"

Ivory nodded slowly.

"Yes. Do you think you can?" she asked. "If you really had to, do you possess the will it takes to stop her? Not detain...kill."

"I don't know," I said. "My brain abhors what she would become. I know, rationally, she must be stopped no matter what."

"And in your heart?" she asked, pointing at my chest. "What do you know there?"

"I care for her," I said softly. "I love her."

"But?"

"But I will not sacrifice those closest to me—my family—for her."

"Then you know what you must do...if it comes to that."

"Can you remove the amethyst?"

"I don't want you to cling to that hope," she said. "The chances of her surviving the removal of the amethyst is slim. She has been merged with it, even if partially; it is part of her now, and she is tapping into its power."

"I know," I said. "It was either that or sacrifice her."

"Do you know what this merging entails?"

"I do."

"I don't think you do," she said. "Removing that gem is similar to losing a major organ. There's a chance the patient can survive, but it's not a good one."

"But there *is* a chance," I said, clinging to the hope regardless. "Even if it's slim, there's a chance."

"Just like there's a greater chance it could kill her," she answered. "You need to be perfectly clear about this. If—and that's a large if—she survived, she would not be the person you knew. Depending on the severity of the separation, she could have no memory of you at all. You won't know the outcome until it has come to pass."

"But she could survive?" I asked. "Even if it means she doesn't know or remember me?"

Ivory gave me a hard look.

"Do you know what you may be asking?" she asked. "You just professed love for this woman."

"Isn't that what love means?" I said. "Being willing to lose what you cherish for another's happiness and well-being?"

"Selflessness and sacrifice, yes," Ivory said. "You could lose her...forever."

"If it gives her a chance," I said, "it's worth it. I'm willing to risk losing her if it means she gains her life."

"You should always be careful with what you request," she said. "It has been my experience that occasionally the worst possible outcome to a situation is getting exactly what is wanted."

"I'll take my chances," I said. "What is the threshold? By when would you need to treat her?"

"If you can get her to me before the final transformation, there is a chance," she said. "Understand that the closer to the transformation you bring her to me, the lower her chances of survival."

"What happens if the transformation has started?"

She gave me a hard look and stared into my eyes.

"You can still bring her to me, but know...she won't be leaving the Tower...alive."

"I understand."

"I truly hope you do," Ivory said, getting to her feet. "If the transformation starts, it would be more merciful for you to end her, than bring her to the Tower. Can you do that?"

"Do I have a choice?"

"No," she said, glancing over at the Rakshasa. "If the corruption is too far gone, she will die a horrible and painful death, but not before she unleashes pain and suffering on everyone in her life. I would imagine she would start with those closest to you. Are you prepared to allow that to happen?"

"No."

She rested a hand on my leg and shook her head.

"I've lived a long, long time and have made many hard decisions in my life," she said, and for a brief moment, her voice sounded old. "I do not envy the choice you face, child."

"Thank you for your wisdom."

She nodded and gave me a tired smile.

"With you, at least, I know some of it will sink into that thick skull of yours," she said, waving a hand in my direction. "Trying to teach your second...eh, too much work."

"I hear that a lot," I said. "Not that anyone besides Char has tried to teach her anything."

"Because Tiger's greatest adversary lies between her ears," Ivory said, pointing to her temple. "Once she overcomes that, she will be open to teaching. Until then, she is at war, which means, sadly, so are you."

"It is foolish to fight a war on multiple fronts," I said, absorbing her words as I flexed my leg. "Speaking of which, how soon will I be able to move?"

"The wounds will be healed in the next hour or so," she said as the Rakshasa moved to the door. "In the future, try and avoid sharp projectiles headed your way."

"I'll do my best."

She looked down at my bandaged arm and leg, and raised an eyebrow at me.

"Your best hasn't been good enough. Do better," she said with a small smile. "Next time, if you insist on getting impaled, get wounded closer to the Tower. You know I hate leaving my home."

"I'll work on it."

"See that you do, and be careful hanging about with that Night Warden," she said. "He's currently carrying—"

"I know."

"Good. As long as you realize the danger you place yourself in," she said. "That goddess is bloodthirsty and insane. If he loses control of her, or she manages to wrest control from him, Regina will be the least of your concerns. Do you understand?"

"I do," I said. "I'm well aware of the danger."

She shook her head and headed for the door.

"Doubtful. Children these days, playing with fire and expecting not to get burned," she muttered under her breath. "Come see me about that mark of yours when you have time.

I doubt Char taught you what it does and doesn't do... Typical dragon."

She left the room with the Rakshasa following silently behind her. As I had guessed, outside the door stood another Rakshasa. Ivory turned and headed down the corridor. A few moments later, a white flash filled the corridor and nearly blinded me as she teleported back to the Tower.

SEVEN

Tiger and Grey came into the room.

"What did she say?" Tiger asked as she stepped into the room. "Did you *speak* to her?"

"I did," I said. "I asked her to be patient with you and not blast you to tiny Tiger particles."

"How considerate of you," Tiger said, crossing her arms. "What else did she say?"

"She called you impossible to teach, but realized that you were just a child that required some moments of stern discipline."

"What?"

"And that she was willing to dole out a measure of pain extreme enough to facilitate jumpstarting your brain into accepting new information," I said. "She even thought it would be possible to teach you new things...imagine that."

Grey chuckled and looked away when Tiger shot him a look.

"She said *what?*" Tiger asked, glaring at me. "Did she just call me stu—?"

"Difficult," I answered, cutting her off. "She called you difficult but not impossible."

"Fine, I can accept that."

"She also gave her word not to blast you into oblivion for being, well, being you."

"She gave her word?" Grey asked. "You got her to give you her *word*? Ivory? From the Tower?"

"Is there another I'm not aware of?"

He narrowed his eyes at me.

"How?" he asked. "She's an ifrit. They don't give their word easily...or ever. Not without a serious trade. What did you offer her in return?"

"What I've always offered her—my friendship."

"Your what? Friendship?" he said, thrown off. "She gave you her word in exchange for your friendship? That's it?"

"Jealous?" Tiger asked. "Seems like she *really* likes him."

"No, not jealous, perplexed," Grey said. "She's not acting like a typical ifrit—maybe she has brain damage?"

"She thinks highly of you too," I said. "Called you insane for bonding to a psychotic bloodthirsty goddess. Other than that, she was quite pleasant."

"She called me insane? Tell me something I don't know."

"And your woman?" Tiger asked. "What did she say about Regina? Can Ivory undo the damage from the amethyst?"

I grew serious.

"There's a chance—slim but possible," I said. "The window is narrow, but I think we can do it."

"How slim and how narrow?" Grey asked. "What do you need to do?"

I explained what Ivory had shared regarding the amethyst.

Grey shook his head slowly, and even Tiger looked disappointed.

"Listen," Grey began, "I know you have feelings for her,

but what Ivory is suggesting...that goes beyond narrow and slim. Are you sure you want to do this?"

"I'm sure," I said. "I'll understand if you want to walk away. No hard feelings and no bad blood between us."

"If this is the path you want to take, I'll back your play," he said, his voice grim. "I've walked this road. It wasn't the same road, but it's similar enough for me to recognize the neighborhood."

I glanced at Tiger.

"You know I can't stand her," she said. "But she was one of us once, and for some insane reason you care for her. Wherever you go, the Directive goes, you know that. If that means we try and save your psychotic woman, then we'll try and save her."

"Until you can't," Grey said. "There is a chance this amethyst will corrupt her beyond even Ivory's reach. You know this, right?"

"I do," I said. "Either of you can decline to assist me in this, but I *will* stop her and remove the amethyst from her."

"And if you can't?" Tiger said. "What happens if you can't remove the amethyst?"

"He knows what must be done if he can't," Grey said, his voice hard. "Are you prepared for *that* outcome?"

"Yes," I said, my voice equally hard. "I'm prepared for every eventuality."

"I said the same thing," Grey replied. "I was wrong."

"What if it changes her?" Tiger said. "What if you manage to get it out of her and she changes into someone else, someone you don't recognize, or worse—someone who doesn't recognize you?"

"Ivory mentioned that there is a chance of that happening," I said. "If it means she gets to survive without trying to kill everyone, I'll take that as a win."

"Will you?" Grey asked. "I'm asking, because when I faced

that choice, I had a hard time accepting the loss. In fact, I couldn't accept it to the point I cast an entropic dissolution in the city, trying to save my Jade."

"I'm not you, Grey," I said. "If Regina survives the removal of the amethyst, but loses all recollection of me, of us, I can live with that."

"You're stronger than I was," Grey said.

"Would you do it again?" Tiger asked. "If you had to—?"

"I said *was*," Grey answered with a low growl. "If I had to do it again, I would give Jade the easiest death possible."

"You would?"

"I'd make the most of what little time we had left, not squander it away, looking for an impossible cast to revert her condition, risking an entire city trying, and failing to save her, while dooming myself."

"You did what you thought was best."

"It was wrong. Sometimes, the best way to demonstrate your love is to let that person go," Grey answered. "I was young, foolish, and worse, selfish. I thought I was trying to save her for her."

"You weren't," I said. "You were doing it for…"

"Me," he said. "I didn't want to lose her because I didn't want to be alone. We all know how well that worked out, considering I'm the last Night Warden."

"Shit, Grey, I'm sorry," Tiger said. "I didn't know."

"No need to be sorry," he said with a small smile. "There was no way you *could* know, unless you were there, or are one of the few unlucky I call a friend."

"I consider myself fortunate to call you my friend," I said. "You may be a colossal pain"—I glanced at Tiger—"but I'm somewhat immune to massive pains in my life."

"You seem intent on walking a path that is going to lead you to massive pain," she said. "Keep it up."

"I'll tell you why I'm walking this path with you, Eyes,"

Grey said, staring at me. "When the moment came to make the choice, I faltered. I made it, but I faltered when it mattered most, and it cost me...everything. I don't want that to happen to you."

"Thank you," I said. "I know this must be difficult for you. To revisit this wound and pry it open again—"

"Not a picnic, no," he said. "Also, Maledicta is still roaming the streets of my city. Your dragon plans on using them or letting them roam the streets. That's not good for anyone. They need to be retired. Permanently."

EIGHT

"We may have a larger issue there than I imagined," I said. "Maledicta's second is a giant named Mura, whose size belies his ability and agility."

"Mura?" Grey said. "Did you say Mura?"

"Yes," I replied. "He's enormous, and—"

"Fast," Grey finished. "Built like an ogre, but insanely light on his feet."

"He scaled a wall in seconds," I said. It had been impressively frightening. "No one that large should be able to move that fast."

"I swear if your next sentence is that he's able to leap tall buildings in a single bound, or he's faster than a speeding bullet, you will recover from your wounds while unconscious," Tiger warned. "We've faced worse things than large assassins who can move fast. Please."

"In any case, he's Regina's second in Maledicta, though I have the suspicion he really leads the assassins and is humoring her for reasons of his own."

"Power, most likely," Grey said. "With Regina, Maledicta has access to Cynder's network. I wouldn't put it past the dragon to use the group until Regina and the rest of the assassins are no longer useful. We are expendable to dragons like her."

"Char doesn't act like that," Tiger said. "At least I've never seen—"

"Don't kid yourself," Grey said. "Who do you think taught Cynder? They don't go to some Dragon Academy of Cruelty and Death. Char helped shape Cynder to be the dragon she is today."

"She's never been cruel toward me," Tiger said, glancing at me, "Toward us. She has always treated us with respect."

"You haven't crossed her...yet," Grey said. "She is not your friend. She may have given you her mark—it means nothing, less than nothing, if it comes down to sacrificing one of you and saving her blood kin. The sooner you learn that, the better. She will choose dragons over humans every single time. Don't forget that."

"Everyone is an enemy, until proven otherwise?" Tiger asked. "Is that the Night Warden credo?"

"You're not nearly old enough to question me or the Night Wardens, *cub*," Grey answered. "For the record, that's not the Night Warden credo, that's *my* credo. It's one of the only reasons I'm still here to talk about it. You'd be wise to adopt it, considering the circles you're moving in these days...Charkin."

"Cub?" Tiger said. "Did you just call me—?"

"Yes, now stay on task," Grey snapped. "If you want to release some of that pent-up aggression, feel free. We have an assassin group on the streets, being led by a corrupted blademaster, who is in turn under the impression that she can face-off against of all things, a dragon. You know what I call that?"

"What?" Tiger said. "A clusterfu—"

"A target rich environment," Grey finished with a wicked smile. "We'll do our best to save Regina. That's the priority.

Hopefully, we can deliver her to Ivory within the time needed, but that still leaves Mura, Maledicta, Cynder, and her Nine to be dealt with."

"They all pose a significant threat individually," I said. "Collectively, this is potential suicide."

Tiger smiled.

"Only if they try and stop us," she said. "We get Regina to Ivory and stomp the rest of them out of business."

"You ever face a dragon…to the death?" Grey asked. "I'm not talking about those lovefest sparring sessions you have at the Dungeon, where Char takes it easy on you."

Tiger's expression grew dangerous.

"Grey…" I started, but he raised a hand.

"I need to know who has my back. Sparring is not fighting for your life. Yes or no?"

"No," Tiger said. "Not in a life or death situation."

"I appreciate the honesty," Grey said with a nod. "When it comes down to it—*if* it comes down to it—you leave Cynder and her Nine to me. She will cut through you with such speed, you'll still be wondering what happened as your limbs violently leave your body."

"You think you can face Cynder and her Nine?" Tiger asked, incredulous. "Alone? Now I know you've lost your mind. I know for a fact, Haven has a supernatural Psych Ward, maybe we should give Roxanne a call so she could accommodate you?"

"No, thanks," he said with a small shake of his head. "Rox doesn't feel comfortable when I'm there for more than a few hours, despite her attempts to restrain me 'for my own good'."

"Rox?" Tiger asked. "Really?"

"We go back a while," Grey said. "I just don't enjoy Haven's hospitality, and she worries too much. If it were up to her, I'd probably be a permanent resident."

"That does sound like Roxanne," I said. "But you can't possibly think you can face off against Cynder and her Nine?"

"Like I said," Grey said, "if it comes to it, you leave Cynder and her dragons to me. You focus on getting Regina to Ivory before she transforms into something much worse than what she currently is, and we all have to stop Mura and Maledicta."

"How much of a threat is this Mura?" Tiger asked. "Maledicta I have an idea about, but I've never heard of this Mura."

"I have a feeling you'll meet him soon enough," Grey said. "Then you can formally introduce yourself."

"Hilarious, old man," Tiger said.

"It's not like you would be scared or anything?" Grey asked. "That wasn't a question born out of fear?"

"I don't do fear," Tiger said. "It's wise to know who you will face in battle. Especially when I may have to save geriatric mages who may stumble in the middle of their casts. Know what I mean? Are you certain you *can* cast? Has the arthritis started kicking in, making the gestures difficult?"

"You know what? I'll let you have first crack at Mura when we run into him," Grey said. "It will be my honor to see how the younger generation deals with a threat like him. I look forward to the lesson you will share...*sensei.*"

"I'll take it slow, so you can keep up."

"I appreciate that," Grey said, looking at me. "How long before you're mobile?"

"A few hours."

"That works," he said. "I need to head down to the Dive. When you're ready to move, meet me there and we'll locate Maledicta first. The sooner we remove them from the field, the easier this will be."

"There is no description of this situation where I would use the word 'easier'."

"Context is decisive," he said. "Easier than, say, facing Mura and a mob of assassins. See? Now it makes sense."

"Only in your mind," Tiger said. "For the record, no one is getting in your Deathmobile."

"Her name is The Beast, by the way," Grey said. "And I wasn't expecting it. She's pretty picky about who she lets ride her. How would I explain your deaths to the rest of the Directive? See you in a few hours."

He smiled and left the room.

NINE

Tiger gave me a look as Grey left the room.

"This is a bad idea," she said. "He's certifiable."

"If I'm not mistaken, I'm fairly certain that being certifiable is one of the primary qualifications for acceptance as a Night Warden."

"I'm serious, Seb, he has a bloodthirsty blade capable of siphoning life force or energy or...something," she said. "It's dangerous, *he's* dangerous."

"He's also a friend, a good one."

"Those two aren't mutually exclusive," she shot back. "He has baggage—the kind of baggage that makes him broken. You heard how he spoke about Jade. He jeopardized the entire population of this city to try and save her."

I gave her a hard look.

"Say what you want to say, Tiger."

"You are not Grey," she said after a pause.

"I'm aware," I said. "Do I appear confused about who I am?"

"Don't be a smartass, you know what I mean."

"Actually, no, I don't," I said. "Why don't you explain exactly what you mean?"

"He unleashed an entropic dissolution in the city," she said. "I know you've done some insane things, but you're not that insane."

"I leave that level of insanity to you and the others," I said with a small smile. "Someone in the Directive needs to be the sane one."

She sighed and looked away.

I knew this was difficult for her; Tiger was never one to easily express or demonstrate her private emotions. She would eventually get to what she really wanted to say, I just needed to be patient.

"It's okay," I continued, "you don't have to—"

"I don't want you to sacrifice yourself trying to save Regina," she said, the words in a rush, then she composed herself. "The Directive needs you...all of us need you here. Alive."

I looked off to the side and let her words hang between us for a few moments. I knew she was expressing her feelings from a place of fear and concern, which was why anger towards her never entered the equation.

"Do you think my life is at risk?"

"You're asking me this while recovering from having two blades in your body," she said, getting angry. "Are you serious right now? She impaled you with *two blades*, and *this* is her showing you how much she *cares*. She's deranged, don't you see that?"

"I do," I said. "With Regina, it's just that she doesn't—"

"I swear, Seb, if you say that she just doesn't know how to control herself or some other rubbish, I'll stab you myself," Tiger warned. "She is totally cognizant of her actions. She *chose* to stab you. These attacks weren't accidents."

"She could have buried those blades in my neck, you know."

"I do know—I know you sound like an abuse victim," she said, glaring at me. "Are you saying she only stabs you because she loves you so much? Are you listening to yourself?"

"It's complicated," I said, my voice hard. "Despite all appearances to the contrary, my life is not at risk...from her."

"You're delusional," she countered. "With Regina, *all* our lives are at risk, but especially yours, you just never see it or choose not to. At this point, I'm beginning to wonder if you *even* can see the danger you're in."

"I'll share something with you no one in the Directive knows," I said. "When Regina demanded I choose between the Directive and her, I chose the Directive."

"Really," she said, giving me a look that said I was being beyond obvious. "I hadn't noticed since you stayed and she left, violently. Newsflash, everyone in the Directive knows this."

"Of course, but what none of you know is *why* I stayed," I said. "I never explained my motivation for remaining with the Directive. Not even Regina understood that the Directive is my family. If she had, she would have never asked me to abandon all of you."

"You don't need to explain your motivation to me or any of us in the Directive," she said. "What matters is that you stayed."

"I know."

"It looks like she's not asking this time," Tiger said, looking and pointing at my wounds. "These wounds look like you either go with her, or you get dead."

"She alluded to as much," I said, shifting my leg. The bandage around my thigh felt extra tight. "If we can unmerge the amethyst from her, we can return her life to her."

"What if she doesn't want the amethyst removed?" she asked. "Power is a tricky thing. People get a taste and sometimes they don't want to give it up."

I nodded.

"Some will sacrifice everything for power," I said. "Unfortunately, I don't think she's going to relinquish the amethyst willingly."

"Really, Sherlock? What gave it away? Was it the first or second blade she buried in you?" Tiger asked, shaking her head. "Or was it the mob of assassins she now controls? Maybe, just maybe it's the gaping hole we now have in the side of the Church?"

"All of the above, but more than that it was our brief conversation," I said. "She claimed Maledicta as hers and vowed to take down Cynder and the Nine."

"She plans on taking down not one but ten dragons?" Tiger asked, her voice filled with awe. "On her own?"

"Well, she has Maledicta and that mountain, Mura," I said. "She may last one or two minutes."

"Seconds is more like it," Tiger said. "She thinks she can stand against Cynder?"

"She thinks she's as strong as Cynder, if not stronger."

"Shit, she's going to die...horribly."

"My thoughts exactly, if we don't get her to see reason."

"Are you out of your mind?" Tiger said. "How are you going to make that happen? She's already dead, she just doesn't know it yet. Even I wouldn't go up against Cynder, and I'm not exactly what you call stable of mind."

"True."

"You didn't have to agree so quickly."

"Merely stating the obvious," I said. "Tiger, I have to try... even if this is a doomed op. She was one of us once, and I still—"

"I know, but you are not going to get anyone in the Directive killed to save your sociopathic, homicidally deranged harpy," she said. "This is me, you, and that psychotic Night Warden. No one else is invited to this party."

"The three of us against all of Maledicta and a blade-master who has recently become a near Archmage?"

"I almost feel sorry for them," she said with a twisted grin and tapped the bandage on my leg, causing me to groan with pain. "I'm going to go get the Tank ready. You still have some time before you can move. I'd use this moment to formulate something resembling a plan."

"Don't die?"

"That's an actual thigh slapper," she said, slapping my wounded leg again, this time harder. I glared at her and forced myself to refrain from grunting in pain. "Want to try again?"

"I'll think of something," I said, moving my leg away from her. "Taking advantage of a wounded man when he's down is uncalled for."

She headed to the door.

"Seb, we're the Stray Dogs—we don't fight fair, we take every advantage presented to us and exploit it," she said sweetly. "All that matters at the end of the day is that we go home alive. Your words, not mine."

"No need to take me so literally."

"Only way I've managed to stay alive this long," she said, opening the door. "I'll be back once the Tank is ready. Then we'll head over to Grey's Dive."

"Sounds excellent, I'll prepare the framework of a plan," I said. "I have just the person to consult on surviving this situation."

"You do? Who?"

"You don't want to know."

"Now I want to know even more," she said, stopping at the door. "Who are you going to consult? Char won't help us —not against Cynder—nor will any of her people. That's a dead end."

"I wouldn't dream of asking Char for advice on this," I said. "For all I know, she's complicit in this somehow."

Tiger nodded.

"She is a dragon after all, it's not impossible."

"No, Char is out of the question. Despite the fact we bear her mark, we can't involve her directly in this," I said. "We have to stay closer to home on this."

"Ugh, not the Terrible Trio?" she asked. "I'm not a fan of our city becoming a smoking crater. Those three are fast becoming a nuclear option. Tell me you're not calling the Montague & Strong Detective Agency?"

"No, they only seem to have two settings: cataclysmic and apocalyptic," I said, shaking my head. "I need a master strategist and tactician. Someone who can look at this entire situation and see all the moving parts and suggest a solution that will neutralize Regina and Maledicta, and deal with Cynder and her Nine."

"You know someone like that?" she mocked. "Because we could have used that person a few times recently."

"Are you saying my plans are flawed?"

"Flawed is such a strong word, I prefer riddled with holes and implausibilities," she said. "Who are you consulting?"

"Dexter."

"Like this?" she said, pointing to my wounded state. "He's going to read you the riot act. I thought you didn't want him to know you were banged up and manhandled like an apprentice mage just out of training?"

I shot her a glare.

"Really?"

"Calling them like I see them," she said with a shrug. "You didn't see at least one of those blades coming at you? Were you stunned into blindness by her beauty?"

"That's not what happened and you know it," I protested. "I was distracted."

"With your discipline, that's worse," she said, shaking her head. "Dexter is going to chew you up and spit you out."

"I know, which is why I was reluctant to have him informed initially."

"But you want him to know *now*," she said. "Is this a sudden onset bout of masochism?"

"It can't be helped," I said. "Time is not a luxury we can afford. The longer we delay, the riskier it gets for Regina, and he has information I need."

"Information you need?"

"The less you know, the better, trust me."

"This sounds like all kinds of horrible," she said. "What are you going to ask the Harbinger of Death?"

"Are you sure you want to know?"

"No, I absolutely do *not* want to know," she answered. "Which means I definitely should know. Tell me."

"He knows a stasis darkcast."

"Oh hell, Seb," she said. "Are you insane? A darkcast?"

"If I can cast it, I can make it easier for Ivory to execute Regina's separation from the gem," I said. "I don't need the entire cast, just the stasis aspect."

"Why would he even show you this cast?" she demanded. "You're not a darkmage."

"He was going to show it to me some time back, and I refused."

"Because you had sense then," she said. "Apparently, you are brain damaged now and have lost what little sense you possessed."

"Because I feared the cast back then," I answered. "I was young and didn't think I could execute it correctly. It was too strong and required...it required life-force."

"This just gets better by the second," she said. "So you're saying this cast can kill you too?"

"Only if I cast the entire thing—"

"You said it uses life-force."

"The life-force component would be required if I unleashed the entire cast, but the stasis aspect only requires the first part of the cast," I said. "If I learn that part, I can use it to capture Regina before she does any more harm. We can take her to Ivory before the entire transformation takes effect."

"Or you can screw up, and kill her and yourself in the process."

"Thank you for the vote of confidence."

"You are not a darkmage," she said. "I have no confidence in you executing a darkcast successfully...none whatsoever. They take years to learn, much less master, and you want him to give you the Darkcast for Dummies version?"

"We aren't going to be able to stop her in time to get to Ivory, not without help," I said. "Grey is strong, but Regina also has that Mura giant and the rest of Maledicta. She can keep throwing bodies at us until it's too late."

"Seb...you know the Ivory option is slim at best, right?"

"I know, but it's an option, and I intend to use every option we have available," I said. "Even if it's minuscule, I'm attempting it."

"Fine. I'm with Grey on this one. I'll back your play, but if I see your life is on the line, I'm not letting you sacrifice yourself for her," she said, her voice serious. "You saw her today, she's not looking to be saved, she's looking to burn it all to the ground and give you a front row seat."

"I don't intend to let her succeed."

"Some people and situations are beyond our, *your* control," she answered. "You want my opinion?"

"Not particularly, I'm aware of your opinion."

"I'm going to share it with you anyway," she said, "because I'm generous like that."

"How fortunate for me," I said with a small sigh. "Please, do share."

"Regina is on a collision course with self-destruction," she said, pointing a finger at me. "And she's looking to take as many as she can down with her. We are not joining her for a trip to Annihilation Station. Yes, we are going to try and help her. If we can't, we are getting off the crazy train with extreme prejudice. Do I make myself clear?"

"Crystal."

"Good, get this disaster sorted with your uncle, come up with a plan that isn't suicidal, and I'll be back once I have the Tank ready."

"Will do."

She gave me a curt nod and left the room.

I sank my head back in the pillow and let out a breath.

I focused my mind and prepared to contact my uncle Dexter.

TEN

I wasn't looking forward to speaking to my uncle.

It wasn't because I disliked him—I respected and cared for him considerably. It was just that he came across at best, as disconcerting; some of the stories about his escapades with the Morrigan would make even the most jaded listener blush. These were stories he enjoyed sharing once he realized they made the listener uncomfortable. At worst, he exuded a deep and penetrating aura of terror.

He was, after all, in a relationship with the Morrigan, with all that that entailed.

I had heard the stories of his time as the Harbinger; none of them were pleasant or made for easy listening. There were times I tried to find the middle ground with him, a place somewhere between the lewdness and the dread, but it wasn't always easy.

Despite how difficult he could be, deep down, past all of it, I knew he cared for me tremendously.

His expression of that affection could be described as bluntly uncompromising. The fact that I was a Treadwell never made a difference to him, unlike some of the other Montagues, and for that, I was eternally grateful to him.

To him, I was family, and he viewed me as such, making no distinction between the two family names. We were all one family with multiple branches.

I became grateful for his treatment when I grew old enough to appreciate it; when I was younger, I had resented him for quite some time, until I had seen how he treated the Montagues.

If it was possible, he was even worse with them when it came to training and teaching them casts. Tristan had, on several occasions, received treatment that could only be described as brutally cruel. In those moments, I felt better until I realized that Dex had learned about my discipline and had singled me out for what he called 'special instruction'.

His lack of distinction between the branches of the family had become a double-edged sword. He made it a point to be as harsh and demanding with me as he had been with any of my relatives.

That period of my life was a nightmare.

Even though teleportation wasn't one of my strengths—I certainly wasn't up to his standards in the discipline, and I doubted anyone could match his skill in the casting and manipulation of teleportation circles—I did learn to understand the intricacies of spatial transport while I studied under him.

It turned out that teleportation itself was versatile in ways I could never have imagined and most mages missed. I stopped seeing it as merely a discipline to move an object from one place to another.

He taught me how to merge teleportation with my truesight. Coupled with it, I could utilize my vision to see trajectories of runic passage. In essence I could learn to *see* streams of runic energy unlike any other mage.

I shook myself out of my thoughts and returned to the present. It had been some time since I had learned the family signal. Initially, it was only taught to the Montagues, but Dexter did away with that, claiming that there was strength in unity between the branches of the family.

He made it a point to teach it to the entire Treadwell side of the family, and if I wasn't mistaken to some others that were neither Montague nor Treadwell. I had it on good authority that several of the members of the Fairchilds were privy to the signal as well.

I flexed my fingers and ran over the signal gesture in my mind. It had been years since Dexter taught it to me, and I had had no reason to use it prior to this moment.

It required two hands, which would prove difficult with a wounded arm. I modified my position as best as I could to facilitate its execution.

Getting it wrong would result in some special chastising from my uncle who wouldn't hesitate to let me know I had made errors in recreating the cast.

I walked through it slowly, partly because it had been so long ago, and partly because I was wary of not making a mistake. After a few practice runs, I managed to execute the special gesture. Dexter had taught it to me as a precaution when he realized where my path would take me.

I still recalled his words when I told him that I appreciated the knowledge, but I would never use or need it.

You say that now, but we're family, lad. There may come a day when you need help or advice. It would pain me greatly if you didn't avail yourself of the resource that is your uncle. Besides, I'm much older than you, and you should always heed the wisdom of your elders. Better to have it and not need it, then need it and not have it.

I learned the gesture begrudgingly because even though I had my own streak of stubbornness and pride, it was unwise to deny my uncle when it came to family matters.

I may have been stubborn and somewhat proud, that didn't mean I enjoyed avoidable pain. In the end, it was smarter to learn it, even though I had personally vowed never to use it.

I was thankful now; his foresight had been wise indeed. The gesture formed a special symbol in the air that served as a signal of my desire to speak to him. It was a green rune of power, specifically designed and linked to him.

From what he told me, the power of the symbol would reach him wherever he was, hence I was only to use this symbol when it was absolutely necessary, a dire emergency, someone I cared about was dying, or my own life was in mortal danger—preferably all of the above.

The situation I was facing wasn't life or death—yet. I did feel his insight would be instrumental in my forming my next steps, plus he had something I needed, if I was to stop Regina without spilling blood.

The darkcast.

I just had to convince him to teach it to me.

The symbol pulsed in the air, hovering over my bed and casting the room in a vibrant green light. I didn't know what to expect, since I had never used this method of contact before.

I thought it would create some kind of portal that would allow two-way communication of some sort. After a few moments of nothing, I extended my arm to undo the symbol, when I felt his presence.

"Someone better be dying for you to use that symbol, lad," I heard his voice all around me. "Give me a moment, I'll be right there."

"You'll what?" I said, slightly panicked. "There's no need for—"

A portal opened at the foot of my bed, allowing me a view of what appeared to be a series of an older group of buildings resembling a university campus. My uncle stepped through the portal and into my room.

The portal closed silently behind him.

"Hello, Uncle," I said, peering behind him. "Where was that?"

"We'll get to that later." He gave me a hard stare and took in the room with a glance. "What happened to you? Actually, it looks more like a *who* happened to you?"

"You look...I want to say chic, but I'm not sure what this look you have going on is," I said, trying to change the subject. "You've gotten some much needed rest, it seems."

"You, on the other hand, look like hell," he said, shrugging an enormous crow off his shoulder and pointing across the room. "Go sit over there."

The crow glided over to the far side of the infirmary and perched on a shelf in the corner. Its eyes blazed a deep green as it cawed loudly in my direction.

"What is that?" I asked, surprised at the enormous bird. "Is it trying to speak?"

"Mo says hello," Dexter said, his voice gruff. "That's Herk. He makes himself useful from time to time. Mo wanted to come, but things are happening at the school. One of us needed to remain at the campus. So she sent Herk. He can be her eyes and ears when needed."

My head spun at the barrage of information Dex had just shared. First, he was dressed in some kind of bohemian mage outfit. He wore his long, grayish hair out, an off-white dress shirt covered by a dark green vest waistcoat, finished with a pair of creme loose-fitting linen pants and comfortable leather sandals on his feet.

"School?" I managed when I found my voice. "What school?"

"Like I said...later. You called me," he said, raising an

eyebrow and looking me over. "What happened? Tiger rough you up?"

"I'm quite capable of defending myself," I said. "Why does everyone assume I need assistance in maintaining my well-being? Do I come across as defenseless?"

"Aye," he said with a solemn nod. "From where I'm standing—wounded arm and leg—you don't look so capable."

"It wasn't Tiger," I said, glancing down at my bandages. "She'd never be this gentle."

"This must be your new headquarters." He looked around the infirmary again. "Not bad, I like it, feels grounded. Much better than that sterile office you had before. This place has character and history. So, if it wasn't Tiger, are you telling me this was self-inflicted?"

"Of course not," I said. "Why would I...never mind. It was Regina."

He narrowed his eyes at me.

"Regina, your lady love?"

"The one and the same."

"Lover's quarrel?" he asked, shaking his head. "I'll not meddle in affairs of the heart, it never ends well."

It was best to head him off before this conversation devolved into some sordid story about him and the Morrigan.

"Not a lover's quarrel," I started and explained the situation to him. "How do I approach this? You have some unique experience with phenomenally deadly women in your life. I was hoping you could provide me with some insight on how to deal with her."

He glanced over at Herk before he answered.

"Your words *are* true," he said with a short nod, while still looking at my bandages. "The difference being that the phenomenally deadly *woman* in my life isn't trying to actively end it. Yours seems like she wants to shorten your years on this earth. Tell me what happened."

I brought him up to speed, sharing what had happened with Regina, and the amethyst.

"After merging with the amethyst, Regina is becoming unstable."

"Becoming? You mean more than before?"

"More than before, yes."

"Did she give you a reason for this attack?" Dex asked. "One that made some sort of sense?"

"When you say 'sense', do you mean in the general definition of the word or made sense only to her?"

"Why did she attack you?"

"Because she could and because she feels I belong with her and not the Directive," I said. "She is going to use her newfound power to prove this to me by eliminating the Directive and showing me that my true place is by her side."

"I see," he said, grabbing a chair and sitting by the side of the bed. "How do you feel about this?"

"What do you mean, how do I feel?"

"Well, she clearly has a unique method of showing her affection for you," he said, pointing to the bandaged wounds. "I take it you are not in agreement with her determination?"

"I vehemently disagree," I said. "I am not sacrificing my family because she has decided they must be eliminated."

"Did she say as much?"

"Yes," I said. "She said she's coming for me and will eliminate the Directive to make it so I don't have a choice."

"Why did you call me?" he said, his voice gruff. "You know what you need to do—"

"Kill her? Is there no other option?"

"Neutralizing the threat doesn't always mean killing."

"Well, you made it sound like you were implying elimination."

"Why are we jumping right to the killing?" he said. "Once you go there, it's impossible to come back. I mean, yes, there's always necromancy, but that's a nasty business. Trust me, that's not a path you want to travel."

"Agreed, I'd prefer to postpone the ending of her life for as long as possible, if not indefinitely."

"There are alternatives," he said. "Have you tried speaking with her? You know, having an actual conversation like two adults?"

I pointed to my arm and leg.

"Didn't exactly turn out the way I expected."

He nodded.

"Got it, her idea of conversation involves blades and blood," he said. "Judging from the fact that she supposedly cares for you—or those blades would have been buried in other, more fatal parts of you—would you say anger is a motivating force here?"

"Among other things, yes, she resents the fact that I chose the Directive over her when things ended between us."

"From the fresh wounds, I'd say she may still be harboring some ill intent towards you."

"You could say that, yes."

"Looks like she didn't take your rejection too well."

"She didn't. She insisted I join her and leave the Directive."

"I take it you refused."

"I did, despite the fact that I had misused my truesight on her."

"You used your *truesight* on her?" he asked as he stared hard at me. "Are you daft? Did you do this knowingly?"

"I would never do such a thing knowingly," I said. "I had no intention of forming a bond in that way. I was still new to my abilities. I had no idea... It was a colossal error."

"And yet, form a bond was exactly what you did," he said. "Bloody hell, lad, what were you thinking?"

"I wasn't thinking," I said. "I didn't know the extent of my ability when I exposed her to my truesight. I didn't know how strong I was."

"Well, that explains *some* of her animosity towards you," he said. "She's all twisted up inside her mind. That's not a very productive state for peaceful resolutions."

"Not usually, no," I said. "What would you advise?"

"Worst case scenario, you need to kill her, at least before she kills you," he said, his voice grim. "You can't reason with her or appeal to her better nature. She's not in her right mind."

"A little harsh, don't you think?"

"I'm fairly certain you didn't ask for my opinion on this matter to hear me blow smoke in your face," he said, his voice hard. "I don't coddle and try to soften the blow—not when it's a matter of life and death—and make no mistake, this is a matter of life and death. For the both of you."

"I just don't think it's right," I said. "She shouldn't lose her life for merging with this gem, or for what happened between us."

"True. Tell me, where do you draw the line?" he asked. "Are you going to wait until she kills members of your Directive? How about when she explodes another building and this time kills a few innocent bystanders? How do you suggest preventing her madness?"

"I understand that what she is doing is wrong—"

"This is not only a matter of right and wrong—though stabbing you twice is wrong," he said. "She feels justified in her actions. You formed a dangerous bond with her. A bond she wasn't ready for, one you weren't ready for either."

"I'd have to agree," I said. "But there may be a solution."

"One that doesn't involve wholesale slaughter?" he asked. "I'd love to hear it."

I told him about the Ivory option.

He looked pensive and rubbed his chin.

"Is Regina willing to hand over this amethyst without violence?" he asked. "Is she willing to surrender?"

"Unlikely. It means giving up her new power," I said. "I have yet to see that happen when a mage and power is involved. Not even the most well-intentioned individual willingly relinquishes power in my world, not when it can give them an advantage over others."

"Aye," he said, shaking his head. "You've hit the nail right on the nose. You're going to have to subdue her in order to get Ivory to treat her. Can you?"

"I'm going to need to use deadly force without killing her," I said. "It's the only way I can weaken her enough to capture her."

"That is a dangerous ploy, lad," Dex said. "One miscalculation and she's gone, not injured...gone. Do you understand what needs to be done? What Ivory needs to do?"

"I do."

"You realize Ivory may not be able to undo the merging? That Regina will fight her, and if she's transformed, it will be nearly impossible to save her?"

"But there's a slim chance, Ivory said there's a slim chance if we get to her in time," I said, hoping against hope. "I have to try."

Dex shook his head and rubbed his temple.

"Heavens save me from hungry hellhounds and hopeful mages," he said, looking up. "Why am I here, lad? Why did you call *me*?"

"The stasis darkcast."

ELEVEN

He gave me a hard look and shook his head slowly.

"No," he said, his expression dark. "Out of the question. You don't know what you're asking."

"Not the entire cast, just—"

"No," he said. "You don't have the experience or the skill to cast that without killing someone—and by 'someone', I mean you."

"I just need to learn the first half of the cast, the stasis aspect," I said, my voice matching his. "You were willing to teach me the *entire* cast when I was younger."

"If you had stayed with me while you were still learning, aye, I would have taught it to you," he said. "I had some say over your studies back then, could help and direct you. Now, it would be a death sentence."

"Why? I'm stronger now," I said. "I can learn half the cast."

"The fear," he said. "It's taken root by now."

"I don't fear it."

"You can lie to yourself—and while I may have been born at night, it wasn't last night—I see right through your words, lad," he said. "Did you think I didn't see the fear in your eyes when I first showed it to you? How you reacted? You practically ran away."

"I'm past that," I said. "I was a child when you first showed it me."

"You're saying the fear is gone?"

"Yes, the fear is gone."

"Then why did you request to learn only *half* the cast?"

"I'm not a darkmage..."

"Who said you were?" he looked around. "Anyone here call you a darkmage?"

"It's a darkcast," I said. "In order to execute the entire cast properly, I'd have to step fully into the darkness."

"Where did you hear that?" he snapped. "Who fed you that pile of rubbish?"

"I assumed, it being a darkcast—"

"That's the fear talking, you know, the one you say you no longer feel," he said. "When I first showed it to you, did I ever mention you needing to become a darkmage?"

"No, never."

"Did you think I would have a young mage in my care go dark?" His words were heavy with pain and anger. "Just so he could learn a cast?"

"I meant no offense, uncle."

"It wasn't a rhetorical question, boy."

I felt the energy of the room intensify as he stared at me.

"I meant no insult," I said. "I only merely wanted to point out—"

"Answer the question."

"No, I don't think you would have a young mage go dark to learn a cast," I said. "Not then and not ever."

"I have one more question for you, and I want you to ponder on your words before you answer," he said and formed Nemain, his mace-axe weapon. The energy signature shifted and became oppressive, as an aura of power filled the room. "Do you consider me to be a darkmage?"

I was no longer before my uncle but a powerful mage of staggering power. I had no way to quantify this level of power; all I knew was that he was phenomenally strong. Strong enough to undo my existence with little effort, yet despite all of that power, I felt no darkness, just raw power.

"No," I said, certain in my response. "I sense no darkness in you."

"That would be because I'm not a darkmage, child," he said, disappearing his weapon and allowing me to breathe easier. "Being a darkmage means a lack of balance."

"Did you really have to bring out Nemain?"

"Of course," he said with a wicked smile. "That weapon puts fear in the heart of everyone who sees it, everyone except Mo, of course."

"Are you saying that my thought process is born in fear?" I asked. "That's why I asked for half the cast?"

"You only *think* you don't fear it," he said, pointing at me. "Even your request is formed in fear. How do you expect me to teach you *half* a cast? That's the most daft thing I've heard today."

"I figured it would be possible—"

"It's not," he snapped. "Especially not with a darkcast."

"It doesn't exist or it's not possible?"

"How many halfcasts do you know?"

"None."

"You only ask for half because you fear the *entire* cast," he said. "You try and execute half a darkcast with fear and doubt in your heart and it would be easier for me to end you now. If you want to know the stasis darkcast, you have to learn the entire thing."

"And the fear?"

"Overcome it," he said. "The truly powerful mages act in spite of the fear they may feel. You think I don't feel fear?"

"I've never seen you exhibit fear."

"And because you've never seen it, it must not exist?" He asked. "How arrogantly mage of you."

"I meant, I have seen you stand against threats that would have undone other mages," I corrected quickly. "In those instances, I saw no fear in your behavior or words."

"Doesn't mean I didn't feel fear. All you saw me do is what any mage worth his salt does: act despite the fear. I have more to fear than most other mages my age do. There is more of my heart out in the world, than I have any right to enjoy."

"I don't understand, more of your heart?" I asked. "What does that mean?"

"Mo, You, Tristan, Strong, and that overgrown hellhound puppy of his, two young girls who have fast become part of my family, old and new friends who still take a breath on this, and other planes, are parts of my heart scattered far and wide," he said. "Each one a vibrant part of my life, each one a target for my many enemies. Trust me, boy. I am intimately acquainted with fear."

"I never thought about it that way," I said. "Surely, no one would dare rise against the Harbinger?"

"You're not paying attention," he said, his voice soft. "My being the Harbinger is not common knowledge precisely because it puts those close to me in danger. It makes me vulnerable in a unique way, but that's not why you called me here. What will it be, boy?"

"Entire cast or nothing?"

He nodded.

"Entire cast or nothing," he said. "As much as I enjoy seeing you, I have two young mages back at the school that are intent on redecorating the entire place. So I'd appreciate you being decisive about this. The longer I'm here, the greater the amount of repairs I have waiting for me when I get back."

I gave it some thought for close to half a minute.

"The entire cast," I said finally. "Do you think I can wield it?"

"Do you?"

"I don't know."

"Then I will give you this piece of advice," he said, leaning forward. "Pay attention, because the life you save may be your own. If you have any doubt, any doubt whatsoever as to your ability to execute the stasis darkcast, do not cast it. It will kill you if miscast. Do you still want to learn it?"

"That's not exactly encouraging."

"I don't do encouraging," he said. "Don't you know that by now?"

"I do," I said with a nod. "Yes, I still want to learn it, but why, knowing that it's so dangerous, why would you teach it to me?"

"Because you want to save the woman you love, because I think you can cast it," he said. "Because...you deserve a chance and if I can give it to you, then I will."

"Aren't you afraid I may miscast it?"

"Yes."

"But you're still going to show me the cast?"

"Yes. Even against my better judgment."

"Why?"

"It's the fear of every parent, the fear of every adult looking out over a young child," he said. "One day, you have to go out into the world and make your mistakes. We can advise and guide, but you still have to go out, live your life and take your own risks. All we can do is watch you walk your path and hope we did a good enough job."

"Thank you," I said. "Thank you for trusting me with this."

"Save your thanks and take off your shirt," he said. "Before we're done, you're going to wish you hadn't asked to learn this cast. Get ready."

TWELVE

"What...now?" I asked, surprised, as I removed my shirt as instructed. "I'm still injured. Do you not see my wounds?"

"My eyes are in perfect working order, lad. This should take some of the edge off," he said and gestured. A golden glow suffused my body, followed by a calm numbness. I felt myself descend into a cloud of relaxing, but accelerated clarity of thought. "Did you not hear what I said earlier? I have two young mages, Destruction and Mayhem, intent on demolishing the Montague School of Battle Magic."

His voice was at once very far away and too loud.

"You named them Destruction and Mayhem?" I asked. "What exactly is the Montague—"

"Not their names, it's who and what they are if left unsupervised," he said, cutting me off as he traced more symbols in the air. "Even with Mo there, those two are almost impossible to contain."

"What did you do?" I asked. "My mind feels sharp, but my body feels asleep. What was that cast?"

"I'm merely getting you ready for the teleport."

"Getting me ready for the—?"

He raised a hand to silence me.

"When I say this is going to hurt, trust me, the pain is going to be exquisite."

"Just want to say for the record, not a fan of exquisite pain, or any pain for that matter," I said. "Can we skip the part with the pain?"

"Since we don't have the luxury of time to teach you the stasis darkcast methodically, we can't," he said. "Consider this the express method of information transfer."

"The excruciating express method?"

"Yes."

"Are you saying that because we have to do this quickly, speed means pain?"

He nodded.

"Direct and to the point," he said as he gestured one more time. "I like that, yes. Speed means pain."

"I still don't understa—"

"You will," he said. "Your wounds should be healed by now."

I flexed my arm and leg and found he was speaking the truth. Both my arm and leg had healed completely. While part of my body moved at a heightened speed, the rest of me was stuck in slow motion. I still retained a sharpness of thought, though my body moved sluggishly.

"How did you—?"

"No," he said, stopping me. "Another day I will explain that. Today, we deal with an advanced teleportation skill."

"Teleportation skill?" I asked. "Why does my body feel so—?"

"No questions," he said. "Watch, listen, and learn. One day you come visit me in the school, and I'll explain it all to you, but not today, agreed?"

"Agreed," I said with a slow nod. "I feel like my brain is out of sync with the rest of me."

"Not bad," he said, giving me an appraising look. "I cast a temporal lag on you. Your brain is moving a little faster than normal and your body is moving much slower than normal. It will help with the pain."

"The pain?"

"Hush, now some basic concepts to facilitate this transfer," he said, tracing some complicated symbols in the air between us. They hovered, glowing a soft green as they floated above me. "I will make this as simple as possible. I just need you to grasp this general idea to allow for the transfer of information."

I nodded.

"Right, everything is energy," he said. "You, me, everything around us is energy in different forms. Simple enough?"

"Basic tenet of magic," I answered. "Yes, simple enough."

"These symbols hovering in the air right now are just energy in runic form," he said. "In order to transfer the information contained in these symbols into your brain, I will use more energy to transmute them into information your brain can process and absorb."

"How?" I asked. "That sounds impossible."

"Only because you haven't learned it," he said. "Transmutational teleportation is real."

"That's myth," I said, certain in my belief. "No mage has successfully executed a successful transmutational teleport. The theory alone is so advanced that I doubt any mage alive could even understand the runic symbology behind it, except, perhaps, Professor Ziller."

"Certain of this, are you?"

"Not when you ask me like that, no."

"It can and has been done," he said. "Just not very often."

In that moment, I realized that if anyone had managed a transmutational teleport, it had been my uncle Dexter. He smiled and pointed at the symbols floating in front of me.

"That is the stasis darkcast in its entirety," he continued. "Using a transmutational teleport, I'm going to transfer that information into your brain and you will know the cast."

"One second," I said, holding up a hand and having a difficult time processing his words. "If it is this easy, why don't all mages learn their casts this way? Why do I feel like I want to float away?"

"It's the effect of the cast," he said. "Try to remain still and focus. So far, there is only one person I know besides myself, that can do this successfully and is *willing* to try it. Also, at no point in time did I ever say it would be *easy*."

"If I may ask, who is this other person?"

"Yes, you may ask," he continued, disregarding my question. "As I was saying, it's not easy—the rate of mortality is high, and the pain threshold required to survive the transfer of information itself exceeds human limits."

"It can kill me and torture me while it does?"

"Good, your brain is actually still functioning," he said. "Yes, it can."

"Is it possible to pick one of the options? If so, I'd like to pass on the death option."

He shook his head and continued.

"The rate of success is quite low, if it doesn't kill the subject of the transfer first," he said. "That being said, I'm looking forward to seeing how you will hold up under the process. Are you ready?"

"No, I'm not ready," I said, shaking my head and making to leave the bed, which he prevented easily with one hand. "How high is the rate of mortality?"

"Not that high. Transmutational teleport has only been tried a handful of times," he said, rubbing his chin. "Never been that many volunteers for it...after the first death."

"I can't imagine why," I said. "How many tried it?"

"Quite a few, actually."

"How many of that group survived?"

"Oh, that was a much smaller group."

"How much smaller?" I persisted, my body may have been sluggish, but my brain was rapidly picking up speed as I realized this procedure had a real chance of ending my life. "I'm noticing a distinct absence of numerical quantities here. It seems we have stepped into the theoretical portion of the conversation."

"I will tell you the numbers that matter," he said. "Every single transmutational teleport I have cast has been successful."

"Prior to the one you're about to cast right now, how many of these teleports have you cast?"

"Two. With a one hundred percent success rate."

"Two? You've only cast this twice? And this other person you mentioned? How many times have they cast it?"

"Successfully?"

"I'm not really interested in the failed attempts," I said. "Yes, how many *successful* attempts?"

"One, but only because he refused to try it again," he said. "I'm sure if I could convince him to try again, he would be successful."

I stared at him in mild shock.

"How long would it take to learn the stasis darkcast properly?"

"One year to learn the cast and two years of practice to get it right," he said, holding up three fingers. "If this transfer is successful, you will have 3 years' worth of knowledge embedded into your brain in under thirty minutes."

"Something about that compression of time sounds off," I said. "Exactly how bad is the pain?"

"What can you feel right now?"

"I don't understand, what do you mean what can I feel right now?"

He smashed a fist into my leg where Regina had wounded me. I looked down at the site of the strike and felt nothing, not even the sensation of his fist hitting my leg.

"I felt nothing."

"Good," he said. "That was the earlier cast I used to heal you. Even with that level of numbness, you will feel this teleport."

For the first time since we started this, I felt fear and shuddered at the thought. How severe could the pain be, that I would feel it through this extreme numbness?

"It's still your call," he said, reading my expression. "You can walk away from this. The numbness will wear off in about an hour, you will be fully healed, and then you can formulate a different plan to save your woman."

"This was the best plan I had."

"Really?"

"Yes."

"Did you give it any real thought?" he asked. "I only ask because the flaws in it are large enough to drive a bus through."

"Are you saying it's not a viable plan?"

"It's thin, in fact the whole plan is thin," he said. "You're going to confront your woman, a blademaster who has upgraded her ability to near Archmage level?"

"Yes."

"In this fight, to the death—at least on her end, I imagine—you're going to somehow create an opening that allows you to use the stasis darkcast, if you dare use it, and hope you're strong enough to immobilize her long enough for you to transport her to Ivory."

"Correct."

"In the hopes that she's not too far gone and that Ivory can remove the gem she has merged with, without killing her in the process? Am I following the plan so far?"

"So far," I said. "I know it seems improbable—"

"You're using that word, but I don't think it means what *you* think it means," he said, shaking his head. "The word you're looking for is inconceivable."

"It can work," I said. "It has to."

"Wishing it so doesn't make it so."

"I know it has flaws," I said. "No plan survives contact with the enemy."

"There are so many things that can go wrong at so many points in this plan, it would be easier to point out the few places where things could go right," he said. "This is a fool's errand, boy. Worse, it's a lethal fool's errand that's likely to get you or members of your Directive killed."

"It can be done," I said. "We start with this stasis darkcast. If I die here, the rest of the plan is moot anyway, right?"

"Well, there is that," he admitted. "If your brain turns to meat slush, you won't be very effective as a mage, or anything else for that matter."

"I'm feeling very reassured here," I said. "Do it."

He nodded and placed a hand on my forehead.

"Just lay back," he said. "This bed has restraints?"

"Yes, you can pull them out on either side of the bed," I said. "Conventional and runic restraints are both available."

"You'd better get your second in here," he said. "I won't be able to have my attention diverted, if you decide you need to break free because the pain is too intense. This teleport needs my undivided attention."

I pressed a button on the side of the bed, and Tiger entered the room a few moments later.

"Dexter," she said with a nod. "It's been some time."

"Yes, it has. You're looking as lethal as ever," he said. "I'm going to need your assistance with a particular procedure."

"You're finally getting him a brain?"

Dexter glanced at me, while Tiger looked from Dexter to me and back to Dexter.

"What exactly is this procedure?"

Dex explained what it was while glossing over the more severe outcomes.

Tiger wasn't fooled.

"Tell me what you're not saying," she said. "Can he die during this *procedure*?"

"There is a risk with every procedure of this sort—"

"Do *not* bullshit me, old man," she said. "We have both danced with death enough times to know all the music. Do not dress it up. Plunge the blade in clean."

"He will not die on my watch," Dexter said, his voice solemn, "but it will appear like it"—he glanced at me—"and he will wish for death many times over."

"That bad?" she asked.

"Worse," he said. "If we could move him to a null space, I would do it, but it would interfere with the numbing cast I placed on him. Without that numbing cast, his mind would shatter from the agony. We will have to risk doing this while I mitigate his abilities as best as possible."

"Mitigate his abilities, meaning?"

"Preventing him from casting while I'm trying not to fry his brain to slurry."

"What do you need me to do?"

"These restraints look sturdy, but I don't know if they are sturdy enough," he said. "You have to make sure I can focus on the cast. Which means I need him as still as possible."

"Why not just knock him out?"

"Can't, this is a transmutational teleport," he said. "I'm going to transfer information into that thick skull of his which means—"

"He needs to be conscious," she finished. "I thought

transmutational teleports were only theoretical thought exercises? At least according to Ziller."

"There is a working model, it's just risky."

"This sounds like the worst of all possible scenarios," she said. "I was going to suggest a light tap to the jaw or temple, but you need him present."

"He won't be present, not with the pain he will be experiencing, but he will be conscious, that is the priority," he said. "Can you do that?"

"What if he passes out from the pain?"

"He won't, sadly."

"You are a scary old man," she said. "How are you going to manage to keep him conscious? You'd have to override the body's natural response. How do you plan on bypassing the vasovagal syncope?"

"You're fairly knowledgable about this," Dexter said. "I imagine you *would* be familiar with pain."

"I specialize in pain," she said. "Especially its administration."

"So I noticed."

"I figure you're using some kind of heightened sensation cast?" she said. "Something that will overstimulate his senses and prevent unconsciousness?"

"It's an ancient cast," Dexter said. "Using an artifact."

"An artifact? Which artifact?"

Dexter gestured and formed a collar made of what appeared to be merged steel and ice. Blue-white frost wafted off of its surface as he placed it around my neck.

It sizzled when it touched my exposed skin. At first, I thought it was burning me, but I didn't smell any burning flesh. I looked down and saw that it had frozen the area it was touching. I felt the weight of the collar on my chest, but other than that, I felt nothing.

"You just walk around with ancient artifacts at your

disposal?" Tiger said, staring at the collar and pointing. "What the hell is that?"

"It's called the *Torc Emada*. It was used as a tool of interrogation, to prevent the mage being interrogated from losing consciousness."

"It's a torture device?" she asked, surprised. "For mages?"

"Torture is a strong word," he said. "It was used during the war to gather information from less than cooperative prisoners."

"So, it was used during torture."

"No, the artifacts and casts we used for torture—"

He looked away for a moment.

"That bad?"

"It's probably better neither of you know the details of that," he said. "What I can assure you is that he won't pass out. He will feel every single agonizing moment of this procedure."

"I'd rather not discuss this any longer," I said, glancing down at the large frozen torc collar on my chest. "Tiger, are you in or out?"

"I'm in," she said, looking at Dexter. "You and this torc thing better not kill him."

"I won't," Dexter said. "Get ready."

THIRTEEN

Tiger leaned over the bed and looked down into my face.

An expression of concern flitted across her face before she composed herself. I had never seen her look at me that way, and it made me uneasy.

"You sure about this?" she asked. "I'm sure you could still bail if you needed to."

"No, but it needs to be done," I said. "This is the best way to get the stasis darkcast, to stop Regina."

"I'm not so sure I agree with you about *best*," she said and began working the restraints on my body. "You do realize you can let the clock run out. The gem will take her out soon enough."

"Tiger..."

"Just saying that's always an option."

"It's not an option and you know it," I said. "If I have to execute a permanent solution, I will, but I won't start with a fatal resolution, not when I can get her to Ivory."

"Ivory may not be able to undo the merge."

"We'll burn that bridge when we get to it," I said. "Make

sure the restraints are tight, and activate the runic components."

She let a hand hover near the steel and ice collar around my neck.

"I'm not enthused about this *Torc Emada* artifact. How is it ice and steel at the same time? More importantly, how is it supposed to keep you conscious?"

"I guess we'll find out, won't we?" I said with a reassuring smile, displaying a confidence I didn't feel. "Don't forget the runic components on the restraints."

"I won't," she said as she touched the symbols etched on the restraints. They took on a violet glow and locked my body in place. "There you go...all set."

I had seen these restraints hold a furious ogre in place. I doubted I could match the ferocity or strength of an ogre trying to escape capture.

The restraints had several securing points: wrists, biceps, and shoulders for the upper body, and ankles, knees, and thighs for the lower. They were designed to prevent leverage. It wasn't impossible to break through them. With enough power, I was certain it was possible.

I just didn't think I possessed enough raw strength or power to tear through them, especially when the runic component was activated.

Dexter looked at the activated restraints and examined them closely before glancing at Tiger.

"I'm curious, what is the restraining force of these?" Dexter asked, pointing at the restraints. "The runic components etched in are force dampeners, right?"

"These things have held an ogre in place," she said, glancing at me. "Sebastian is strong, but he's not *that* strong."

"It can hold an ogre with the runic components in place or without?" Dexter asked, examining the symbols. "I need to know if I should reinforce them before we begin."

"I don't think that will be necessary," I said and Tiger nodded. "Your estimation of my power is greatly appreciated, but I don't think reinforcement will be needed."

"Take a deep breath, lad," Dexter said, placing a hand on my forehead. "Eventually, it will end or you'll die. Hold onto that thought, it should get you through this."

Tiger stared at him.

"That's your pep talk?" she asked. "It will end or you will die?"

"No, that's not a pep talk, it's the truth," he said. "Now, step back for this part. Whatever you do, do not touch the torc unless you want to experience new and nightmarish levels of pain that will melt your brain."

"No, thanks," she said, stepping back. "Will he be able to use this darkcast when this is over?"

"If he makes it through with his mind intact, he will have access to the darkcast," Dexter said. "If he doesn't, well, other questions won't matter at that point, will they?"

"True," Tiger said, her voice and expression dark. "Do your thing, old man, and don't kill him."

Dexter nodded and placed his hands together.

He looked down at me again, took a deep breath and held it. He separated his hands, and placed one hand on my chest and the other on the torc.

The frost of the torc raced up his hand, covering his arm with a thin layer of ice. He kept his gaze focused on me, whispered some words under his breath, his exhalation visible as he spoke unfamiliar words, causing symbols to form and float in the air around us.

He removed the hand from the torc and placed it on my forehead again. He removed his other hand from my chest and placed it gently into the floating symbols of the stasis darkcast that hovered over my chest.

The symbols flowed around his hand, casting their soft

green light around us both. They slowly began to rotate as they moved up my body and hovered over my head.

The symbols began to coalesce and swirl together until they became a solid beam of green light about two inches wide and eight inches long.

The beam of light hovered over my forehead, too bright to stare at directly. I noticed frost from the *Torc Emada* floated up into my field of vision.

"Brace yourself, boy," Dexter said. "This is going to be pain beyond anything you've ever managed to live through. Once we begin, you have to see it through to the end. If I try to stop the procedure halfway through, we'll be burying what's left of you. Understood?"

I nodded and put on a brave face.

Part of my brain scoffed at the idea of mind-numbing pain on a level beyond human tolerance, the other, wiser, saner part of my brain accepted the fact that this entire procedure could very well kill me and braced for the worst possible pain imaginable.

My imagination lacked imagination.

The moment the stasis darkcast descended and touched my forehead, a scream tore through my body.

He was right.

I wished for death almost from the start of the teleport.

FOURTEEN

The first sensation was an intense burning.

It was so extreme that I thought my skin had caught flame and I was currently ablaze on the bed. I looked down at my body, but surprisingly saw no flames.

This was followed by the sensation of a hot knife slicing into my forehead as the stasis darkcast descended. I tried to move my head away from the green light of the darkcast, but Tiger held my head still, preventing me from shifting it away.

Another, more intense burning sensation rose in me, distracting me from the searing pain in my forehead. This new burning sensation caused me to pull against the restraints with all the force available to my muscles as I gritted my teeth and groaned, straining every muscle in my body as I pulled.

The restraints held.

This new, internal burning felt as if my blood had become acid and was currently eating its way through my body, devouring me from within. As the feeling of burning intensified, I began to lose consciousness from the agony.

I sighed in relief as I felt the grip of darkness grab the

outer edges of my vision. Sweet unconsciousness was pulling me under and away from the pain.

That relief was short-lived.

As I felt myself slipping away, a wave of ice-cold energy raced through my body; starting at my chest, it radiated outward driving needles of pain into all my muscles, beating the darkness of unconsciousness away.

I screamed again.

I felt the frigid frost of the *Torc Emada* pulse on my chest. The collar unleashed a brutal reminder that I was going to experience every agonizing moment of this process. The green light of the stasis darkcast descended farther, and my mind was suddenly flooded with images, concepts, gestures and executions of casts.

The sheer amount of information that flooded my brain made me gasp in shock. It was information overflow on a level I had never experienced in my life.

Images were rushing into my mind too fast for me to grasp. They collided one with another as the concepts merged with the gestures, which became symbols, which turned into theories I had no hope of understanding in the moment.

I gritted my teeth and tried to shake my head away from the darkcast.

"Don't fight it, boy," I heard Dexter say over the agony. "Ach, you're wasting your energy. There's nowhere for you to go, even if Tiger wasn't holding you in place."

I inhaled forcibly and tensed against the pain.

There was no way I could keep up with the flow of concepts as it entered my mind. Rather than receiving the information, I felt I was being attacked by it, and I had no defenses against the waves that crashed into my mind over and over.

I felt my body spasm and grow rigid, tensing against the

restraints again as a cold and clinical aspect of my brain observed me having some kind of seizure as a result of the onslaught of information.

It appears I'm going to die from information overload. Death by knowledge, what a novel idea.

For some reason, I thought this was humorous and began to laugh maniacally.

"Should he be doing that?" Tiger asked, concern lacing her voice. "That laughing is creepy. It sounds off, like he's losing his mind."

"Aye," Dexter answered, his voice solemn. "It's either that or scream or cry. He'll be doing all three before this is over. I'll try and accelerate the process, but I can't do much at this point. It has to run its course and it will do so at its own pace."

I saw Dexter raise a hand and hold it next to the green light of the darkcast, causing the light to descend slightly faster. Dexter's face was taut with concentration, and I could see the beads of sweat form on his brow.

Tiger looked worried, and I could see her wrestling with the fact that the procedure had to continue until its end. She couldn't stop it halfway or I was certainly finished.

As she held my head, she mouthed some words I couldn't decipher. It was impossible to focus on any one point for longer than a few seconds, before more pain washed over me.

As more images filled my mind, pain seized the base of my neck and squeezed mercilessly. An all-encompassing pressure gripped my head and crushed my temples.

I screamed again, at least I attempted to, but no sound escaped my lips. The pain was so extreme that it had robbed me of the ability to make a sound.

I started sobbing then.

"Please," I pleaded. "Stop this or kill me, but take this pain from me."

"If we stop this now, we *will* kill you, boy," Dexter said, his words firm and uncompromising. "You have to hang on. Remember why you're doing this. You have people to save. You're not doing this for yourself. There are people counting on you. Are you going to abandon them when they need you the most?"

"I can't...I can't do this."

"You can and you must," Dexter said. "If you fail now, you sentence the Directive, the family you formed, to death. Is that what you want? Do you want their blood on your hands because you succumbed to the pain?"

"No...no."

"Now you know why this isn't done more often," he said with a tight smile. "Go deep within, find a place of calm and hold onto that. Remember this isn't forever, it only feels that way."

A feeling of deep shame descended over me as the faces of the members of the Directive appeared in my memory. I remembered everyone who depended on me.

Every member of the Directive was counting on me, Regina, knowingly or not, was counting on me as well. I couldn't give up no matter how badly I wanted to.

"You have to hold on," Tiger said. "It's only pain, Seb. You can deal with pain, you've dealt with pain, we've all dealt with pain. What's a little more? We're the Stray Dogs, we feast on and live on pain. This can't—this won't—break you. Hold on."

"You're almost halfway there," Dexter said, and I thought that a cruel joke. "Prepare, it's going to get worse."

Halfway there? My resolve nearly broke. Worse? How could it possibly get worse?

The next moment, it became abundantly clear how it could become worse. I felt energy accumulate in my eyes and thought it odd that I would gather energy in my eyes.

"His eyes!" I heard Dexter scream. "I can't move my hands right now, you need to do something to cover them!"

Immediately, I felt a blanket of energy over my face and knew that Tiger had dropped a kinetic shield on my face.

"What the hell was that?" she asked. "He's never done anything like that."

"He has, but he was a young boy when it happened," Dexter said. "I doubt he remembers. Bloody hell, I never thought it would present itself through his eyes. I was a bloody fool not to anticipate that."

"What exactly was that, Dexter?"

"This darkcast has been known to manifest its presence through the strongest aspect of a mages' discipline," Dexter answered. "In his case, it's—"

"His eyes," Tiger finished. "Did it affect his eyes?"

"I don't know yet," he said. "We won't know until it's over."

"Slash me sideways," she said under her breath. "What if it did something to his eyes?"

"Of that, I'm certain," he said. "What exactly that something is will have to wait to be discovered."

I started to panic, because I knew I had my eyes open... but all I could see was a blanket of white.

I had gone blind.

FIFTEEN

"My...my eyes," I rasped. "I can't see."

"I know," Tiger said. "I placed a shield over your eyes and made it opaque."

"I...I didn't know you...you could do that."

"Kinetic casts work better when my enemies can't see them coming," she said. "Black energy was forming around your eyes, and it looked dangerous. So I covered it."

"That...that was quick think—"

"Hush now, boy," Dexter said, shifting his hands to the *Torc Emada*. "You're going to need your strength."

Something in his voice—pity, sadness, and worry intermingled with resignation—made my stomach twist into knots. This was not going to be pleasant.

"This next part...it's going to hurt," he continued. "Let him have his eyes. I want him to see what he asked for. He needs to understand how deep this darkcast goes."

Tiger removed the opacity from the kinetic shield over my eyes. She stared at me for a second, and then pointed down at my body, an expression of restrained surprise on her face.

I followed her gaze with my own.

I saw the same black energy Tiger described erupting from my skin. My entire body was covered in a semi-transparent cocoon of shifting, black energy. It flowed over me as the last of the darkcast descended into my head.

"Brace yourself, boy," Dexter warned. "Tiger, we're near the end, this is where we could lose him."

"What do you need me to do?"

"Keep that cast around his eyes just in case, prepare to hold him in place with as much force as needed, even if you have to break him to keep him still." He looked down at my face. "You've done great so far."

I winced and gave him a look.

"I remember every time you would say that during my training, things would become exponentially worse."

He nodded.

"I know you've been through a hell of pain," he said. "But what have I always told you? When going through hell—"

"Don't stop to take in the sights, keep moving until you get to the other side."

"Aye, you're near the exit now," he said, glancing at Tiger. "Ready?"

She nodded in response, a look of determination on her face.

As the green light dissipated, the cocoon of energy around my body exploded with orange light. It exploded outward for a moment and then reversed direction and sank back into my skin.

I screamed again as this new power filled and flowed through my body. My muscles strained to contain the energy as new strength coursed through me.

It felt as if my skin was being peeled from my bones. My bones raged with intense pressure as they were cracked and remade. Intense pain seared through me, ripping at my core and tearing at my mind until I no longer knew where I was.

I pulled at the restraints with a strength I didn't know I had, tearing one of my arms free. With a scream of pain and anger, I reached out for Dexter.

"You don't need to be conscious for this part," he said, keeping his gaze fixed on my chest, while grabbing my free arm with lightning quick reflexes as he gestured with his other hand. "This will be over before you know it."

Those were the last words I remembered before darkness descended on me.

I was still on the bed when I opened my eyes again.

Tiger's kinetic shield was gone, along with the cocoon of black energy around my body. I tried moving and immediately regretted it.

My body felt mauled.

Every muscle in my body ached. A dull pain pulsed in my head, throbbing every few seconds with a sledgehammer of pain tapping my temples ever so lightly.

The rest of my body wasn't too far behind with most of the pain centered in my chest where the *Torc Emada* had rested. The aftereffects resembled what I imagined it would feel like if I had let an elephant sit on me.

I slowly took a deep breath, wary of any lingering pain. I was sore, but I could breathe without difficulty.

"Welcome back," Tiger said. "You're alive."

"I'm alive," I croaked and winced in pain. My throat felt like I had gargled sand and glass with a sulfuric acid chaser. "Mostly. Feels like Ox used me as a punching bag for one of his practice sessions."

"Welcome back," Dexter said from the side of the bed. "Good to see you on this side. It's safe to remove the restraints, Tiger."

"You sure?" she said from the other side of the bed. "He

ripped through that other one as if it were made of paper. I've never seen anything like that, at least not from him." She glanced down at me. "No offense, but you were scary there for a few seconds. I was seriously considering dropping you out of consciousness."

"For my safety?" I asked. "Thank—"

"For *our* safety, not yours," she said, cutting me off. "You were fine...losing your mind, but fine."

"We were never in any real danger," Dexter assured me. "At least nothing the two of us couldn't handle. Though you did exhibit some abnormal qualities there for a few moments."

"Abnormal qualities?" Tiger said. "He tore through a restraint. A restraint. And don't forget the creepy energy thing with his eyes."

"I'll get to that in a moment, but for now, you can remove the rest of the restraints," Dexter said. "He and I need to speak, and I prefer he be comfortable for this talk."

"Are you sure?" Tiger asked. "If he loses it and rips you in half, don't say I didn't warn you."

"It's safe," Dexter said with a smile. "That wasn't his normal strength."

"No shit," Tiger said as she began undoing the rest of the restraints. "He tore through a restraint meant to hold something as strong as an ogre in place. I really hope he hasn't turned into some kind of weird mage-ogre hybrid. That would be unacceptable."

"Did it...did it work?" I asked, trying not to strain my fragile voice. "Did I learn the darkcast? How long was I out?"

"Several hours," Dexter said, gesturing as golden runic symbols fell gently on my body. I immediately felt better. "How do you feel? Your skin hasn't turned chartreuse, and you're asking coherent questions. Are you feeling an uncontrollable urge to SMASH?"

He pounded a fist into his other hand.

"Not particularly, no," I said, giving him an odd look. "Should I be?"

"Not at all, just checking that you're still you and not some mage-ogre hybrid monster," Dexter said with a small smile. "How are you feeling now?"

"I'm feeling better actually," I said. "I'd prefer to never experience that again in my entire lifetime, if possible."

"There? See?" Dexter said, glancing at Tiger. "He appears to be ogre free."

"Oh, hilarious, old man," Tiger said. "I saw what you did there. If he unleashes his inner ogre, I'm not going to hold back. My preferred method of de-escalation with monsters involves multiple fists to the face." She placed a hand on my shoulder and squeezed, a look of relief on her face. Everything she needed to say she did in that one gesture. "Nothing personal, Seb, but I can't have you losing it while we're out in the field. It's too dangerous."

"I totally understand," I said. "Speaking of, we need to head out to Grey's."

"I'll go get the Tank ready," she said and looked at Dexter. "Thank you for not killing him."

"My pleasure, lass," he said with a slight bow. "You should come to the school soon. I'm sure Mo would love to examine your kinetic abilities, and by examine, I mean test your mettle through combat."

Tiger's eyes lit up at those words.

"I have a feeling we're going to have some bad blood with the dragons before this situation with Regina is resolved."

"Aye," Dexter said with a nod. "You need to have a conversation with Char, and more importantly, Cynder." He paused for a moment, as he looked off to the side. "That won't go well. Dragons don't like being held accountable, especially not by humans."

"That means I'm down one sparring partner."

"You can always ask Ursula," I said. "And I'm sure Ox would be more than willing—"

"No, I need a challenge. That's why Char was perfect. I need to face someone I can cut loose with," she said. "I always have to hold back with them."

"You won't have to hold back with Mo," Dexter said. "In fact, she would feel insulted if you did."

A dangerous smile crossed her lips at that and she nodded.

"I'm going to hold you to that invite, old man," she said as she headed to the door. "Make sure he's one hundred before he gets off that bed."

"Absolutely," Dexter said with a nod. "Thank you for the assist."

"Anytime," she said and gave me another look. "Let's finish this. I'll let you know when I have the Tank."

She left the infirmary.

SIXTEEN

Dexter gestured and I felt a weight lift from my chest.

I looked down and the collar of ice and steel was gone.

"I put it back in a safe place," he said. "It doesn't work as a fashion accessory. Clashes with everything." He glanced at door before turning back to me. "Your second is quite fearsome. I like her. Reminds me a bit of Mo."

"She has her moments," I said, glancing at the door. "No one I would rather ride into battle with by my side than her."

"You chose well," he said. "A kinetic mage in full control of their power is an impressive sight to behold. Deadly, dangerous, and devastating. On the battlefield, they were the best shock troops, breaking through enemy lines and positions fearlessly. They were indeed, the forlorn hope."

"I would never want to face her in battle," I said. "Of that I'm certain."

"Agreed," he said with a short nod. "See that it never comes to pass. That would be a dark day indeed."

I nodded in silent agreement.

"How bad was it?" I asked. "And why do I feel like a group

of ogres played tug-of-war with my body, using me as the rope?"

"I'll not be teaching you any more casts using that method...ever."

"That bad?"

"That risky. It was touch and go there for a few moments," Dexter said. "How do you feel—not physically." He tapped his temple. "Up here. How do you feel in that thick skull of yours, what are your thoughts?"

I closed my eyes and became still, searching my thoughts and taking stock of how my mind felt. I was mentally exhausted but rapidly recuperating. My body felt as if I had slept an entire night and was refreshed.

I was just extremely sore but somehow invigorated. I figured that was Dexter's doing with the golden symbols.

Internally, the stasis darkcast lingered in the back of my mind, hovering on the edges of my thoughts. I knew I could access it if I needed to, but something told me it wouldn't be the most prudent action I could take right now.

"Don't," Dexter said. "I know you can access the darkcast, but don't go near it for a few hours yet."

"How did you—?"

"You must be wary of revealing the darkcast," he said. "Powerful mages and magic users will be able to sense it within you."

"I take it that's a bad thing?"

"Depends," he said with a small shrug. "You move in dangerous circles. Occasionally, it makes sense to reveal that you are more than what you seem. It's an excellent deterrent."

"And other times?"

"It can invite aggression and retaliation," he said, his voice serious. "If you reveal the darkcast to Honor, it could be dangerous, he may feel duty-bound to act. Likewise any high ranking member of the Dark Council, though they may be less reluctant to confront you directly."

"Basically, I should keep it a secret?"

"The less people know about it, the better, and safer," he said. "Even within your Directive, I would keep the knowledge between you and your second. This is a banned cast for good reason."

I closed my eyes for a few seconds. When I did, the images and gestures of the cast flooded my brain.

"It's all jumbled," I said. "The cast is in there." I tapped a temple. "But the information is a disorganized mess."

He nodded.

"It will be for a few days still," he said. "Your brain is still processing the information. Think of it as a computer downloading a program and is now sorting through the cast, fitting it into the body of knowledge you currently possess. It's cross-referencing and correlating the cast with every other cast you know. It takes time."

"That I can understand," I said, flexing my fingers into the gestures that would make the cast, without pouring energy into the movements. "This cast...it's ancient."

"Older than me," Dexter said with a smile. "I trust I've explained some of the limitations of the transmutational teleport to you with this experience?"

"That has to be one of the most efficient and most agonizing way of imparting knowledge known to man," I said. "I thoroughly understand why it's not done."

"There are worse ways, trust me."

"I do and have no wish to learn or discover them."

"Aye, I'm glad you gleaned *some* understanding," he said. "Do you understand the stasis darkcast?"

"It allows me to slow or stop the flow of time around a target," I said. "To allow for neutralization, apprehension, or elimination."

"And?"

"If I opt to stop the flow around a person, I must be conscious of the time involved," I said. "Too long and the person will die."

"How long can a person live on one breath?" he asked. "How long can the brain be without oxygen, before irreparable damage? Do you know?"

"Four to six minutes on the outside," I said, "before permanent brain damage. Is that why this is a darkcast?"

"No, lad," he said with a small shake of his head. "It's a darkcast because it takes life-force to execute this cast—that is forbidden. What else is unique to this cast?"

"It's a shared cast."

He nodded.

"Good, you've done your homework," he said. "One of only three shared darkcasts."

"Three? I thought there were only two?"

"Not enough homework, it seems," he said, rubbing his chin pensively. "A shared cast—tell me what that means."

"It means the effects are experienced by the target and the caster," I said. "Not equally in potency and only as long as the target is alive. If the target perishes during the cast, there is a risk of backlash to the caster. In that case, the caster feels the full effect of the cast."

"Tell me what that means *practically*."

"If I use this cast, I should use it for no longer than one to two minutes," I said, giving it thought. "Longer than that, I risk Regina's life. If she dies while in the cast, I have a very limited amount of time to extricate myself from the cast before dying myself."

"What are the effects to you while you execute it?"

"I feel the effects of slowed time," I said. "Not to the extent she will feel, but I *will* experience it as well."

"For you, the effects are halved—remember that, it's important."

"Effects are halved," I said more to myself. "That allows me more autonomy than the target."

"Twice as much, in fact," he said. "If the target dies, how long do you have?"

"A minute?"

"You wish," he said. "You have approximately thirty seconds. Any longer than that and you have missed the window. What happens if you miss the window?"

"I step into stasis and die shortly thereafter."

"*That* is the real reason why it's a darkcast," Dexter said, his voice somber. "Mages kept getting themselves trapped in the cast, until it was deemed too dangerous, and then banned from all mage curricula in all of the sects."

"It seems so dangerous," I said. "Why did you want to teach it to me at such a young age?"

He gave me a hard look before speaking again.

"Without pouring any life force into it, execute the disabling gesture for the stasis darkcast," he said, crossing his arms. "Go on."

It took a few moments of thought, and then I seamlessly executed the gestures required to neutralize the stasis darkcast as if I had known it all my life.

"That's it. Yes," he said. "A little clunky around the edges, but that's the complete cast."

"That came naturally," I said, looking at my hands in amazement. "As if I had always known it."

"There was no way to share that knowledge with you without teaching you the cast," he said with a satisfied nod. "There are many casts that require you have firsthand knowledge of them in order to combat their use against you."

"The discipline comes from not using them," I said. "Not from knowing them."

"Correct," he said, tapping me on the shoulder. "You don't become a darkmage from knowing the darkcasts. It begins when you surrender to the allure. What is the final component of the stasis darkcast? What really makes it a darkcast?"

I searched my memory for the newly acquired knowledge of the stasis darkcast, until I found what I thought was the answer.

It was chilling.

"If the target dies in the cast, it siphons the life-force of the designated target, transferring that power to the caster," I said. "It's a vampiric siphon."

"Yes," he said. "A mage who abuses this darkcast could grow in power rapidly."

"Wouldn't that be a risky proposition? You'd have to kill the target and then run the risk of death in order to acquire the power from the life-force."

"Those in pursuit of power seldom give thought to such things," he said. "The goal, the prize, is the only thing that matters."

"It's too dangerous to be common knowledge."

"That is the allure and the trap of this darkcast," Dexter said. "That transference of power is why it's a darkcast. If you miscalculate the window of time, you die. What do you think happened to so many mages?"

"They miscalculated and thought they had more time?"

"Yes, I'll give you a basic example, so you can understand."

"Please," I said, slowly wrapping my brain around all this new information. "It's a large amount of information to absorb."

"I understand," he said, holding up a hand. "For example, if a stasis darkcast is held for three minutes, with an outside window of four—hypothetically, since four minutes is quite a long time—and the target dies in the cast, how much time does the caster have?"

"One minute," I said, certain of my answer. "If four minutes is the outside window, the caster still has a minute to disable the cast and remain safe."

"Which is why we would be burying your body along with your target," he said, shaking his head. "Try again."

I searched the cast in my mind, and the realization came to me. *There was an immediate trigger.* If the target died in the cast, the caster only had thirty seconds to exit the cast before it was too late.

This trigger was devised to prevent an overflow of life-force energy into the caster, killing him in the process of transference. To remain longer than the allotted time, trapped the caster.

It was an effective and deadly deterrent.

"Thirty seconds," I said after some time. "There's a fail-safe in the cast to prevent rampant siphoning."

"Thirty seconds," he said, his voice hard. "Remember that. You have only *thirty seconds* from the time of death of the target to the moment you exit the cast. Any longer and what happens?"

"I die."

"Now you're finally understanding what so many failed to grasp."

A voice came over the infirmary intercom.

"Hello, Boss," Rabbit said. "Tiger would like me to inform you that if you've wrapped up your torture session, she's outside waiting in the Tank."

"Thank you, Rabbit," I said. "I'll be out shortly, unless she suggests I exit the infirmary half-dressed?"

"Ew," Rabbit said. "No one needs to see that. Get dressed then head out, and thank you for that nightmarish imagery. Really, ew."

I turned to Dexter.

"Thank you, for nearly melting my brain and imparting

the stasis darkcast," I said. "Most importantly, thank you for keeping me alive."

"I told you…you weren't going to die, even though you would wish it," he said. "You did better than I expected. I wasn't going to let you expire, lad. There was no way I was going to face Magda Treadwell to break her the news of the demise of her favorite grandson. There are some threats even I would not dare face, thank you."

He shuddered at the thought and I smiled. My grandmother's fearsome reputation preceded her with good reason. She had earned the name Magda the Maleficent through her deeds of destruction during the war.

"I understand your reluctance," I said. "Please give the Morrigan my regards. Tiger and I, at the very least, will pay your school a visit in the near future."

"Herk," Dexter said, extending an arm as the huge crow glided over and perched on his forearm gently. "Bring the entire Directive, I'm sure they deserve a real vacation. The school can be quite tranquil. I think it would do you some good. That way you can meet the girls. I'm positive they will make your visit…interesting."

I nodded as thoughts of the choices that lay before me came to mind.

"I'm not looking forward to any of this," I said. "If there were another way—"

"I would be concerned if you *were* looking forward to it," he said. "This isn't going to be easy. It's not meant to be easy, but I know you *will* make the right choice."

He pointed at my hand.

"I see the dragon has given you and your second her mark," he continued. "Do you know how to use it?"

"Ivory promised to show us its workings."

"No offense to the ifrit, but this is a mark she may not know everything about," he said with a smile. "I know Char.

More importantly, I *know* dragons. You need to learn how to disable that mark, you'll thank me in the future, trust me."

I looked down at the mark of the dragon in flight on my hand.

"I do," I said. "Have a safe trip back."

"Always," he said. "Listen to your heart and mind, and make the right choice."

"I will."

He formed a portal.

"I know," he said. "You're my family."

He stepped through the portal, disappearing from sight as it closed behind him.

I got dressed and exited the infirmary.

SEVENTEEN

The Tank was parked outside the Church.

The engine idled with a throaty purr as the sun set on the city. Tiger sat behind the driver's wheel. She had the window rolled down, and her face was set in grim determination.

I took a moment to look over the cleanup of the explosion. The aftermath of the attack was a subdued affair. Most of the EMTes were gone.

Thankfully, there were no casualties from the explosion.

We were lucky—this time.

I didn't think we'd be this lucky next time Regina decided to unleash her anger and flaunt her power and control over Maledicta.

I pulled out my phone as I surveyed the damage and pressed a number.

"Yes," came the soft spoken reply. "I have equipped Tiger with a dossier on Mura. It should be in the Tank waiting for you. I also sent you a digital copy in case you needed to get the information on your phone."

"Rat," I said, surprised, "how did you even know I was going to request a file on him?"

"I have files on all persons of interest, Director," Rat said. "Mura has been in Maledicta's ranks since before Calum took over the position of leadership. He has always wanted power. It only made sense to monitor him and his sphere of influence in the organization."

"Do you have a file on Cynder too?"

"Of course," he said. "Would you like it?"

"Yes, please. No need for a hard copy, just send it to my and Tiger's devices," I said. "One more thing."

"The answer is yes," he said in a soft voice laced in steel. "I have dossiers on everyone in the Directive—everyone."

"Why?"

I knew the answer, but I wanted to hear it from him. I expected this from Rat—it was the reason he was the head of the Directive's branch of espionage and surveillance.

"We are all human and fallible," he said. "All of us. Any one of us can succumb to the lure and temptation of power. Though the probability is low, it is not zero."

"True."

"In the case of that eventuality," he continued, "there may be a time when one of us goes rogue, necessitating neutralization."

"Which would require the remaining members of the Directive to possess a list of strengths and weaknesses of the subject in question, to effect this neutralization."

"Correct," he said. "Every member has an encrypted copy of this file that will open in the event of a particular member's defection and or betrayal."

"Is there a dossier on *you* in this file?"

"Yes. My dossier was the first one I added to the file," he said. "Along with the best method to stop me, should I turn on the Directive."

"I hope that day never comes."

"False hopes are more dangerous than fears," he said, surprising me by quoting Tolkien. "I prefer to rely on the predictability of the human nature. No one is immune, no matter how much they may try to convince themselves. No one."

"I didn't take you for a cynic."

"I'm not," he said. "I'm a realist and I believe in being prepared. Will there be anything else?"

"Regina was behind the attack."

"I know," he said. "I sent you her most recent dossier, as well as the strengths and weaknesses of Maledicta as an organization."

"Thank you," I said. "We'll speak soon."

"We will."

He ended the call.

I headed over to the Tank and sat in the passenger side. I opened the file on Mura on my phone while I took the hard copy and placed it in the large glove compartment. I strapped in and began to read.

"Rat send you that?" Tiger asked as I strapped in. "He downloaded some for me as well. How does he get this information?"

"I don't know, and I don't think he would share if I asked," I said. "Has he ever been wrong with his information?"

"Not to my knowledge," she said, pulling away from the Church and heading south on Park Avenue. "Not once."

"I agree," I said. "He has an excellent record with providing information. He just informed me of something I had long suspected."

"And that is?"

"He has dossiers on all of us in the Directive."

"Tell me this isn't news to you," Tiger said, heading downtown. "Individually, the Stray Dogs are each a force to be reckoned with. Collectively, it's common knowledge on the street, one does not—"

"—cross the Stray Dogs," I finished. "True. Unless the person doing the crossing is or in this case, *was* a Stray Dog."

"Regina knows she crossed a line by attacking the Church," Tiger said as she swerved through traffic. "She has to know we will respond in kind."

"I'm fairly certain she's counting on it," I said. "Is this the fastest way to Grey's?"

"Yes," she said. "I do know *my* way around *my* city, thank you."

I raised my hands in surrender.

"Just asking."

"Don't," she said, nearly removing the rear bumper on a taxi as she cut off another driver and nearly sideswiped two others. She gave me a quick glance and smiled. "That's called defensive driving, in case you were wondering."

"I was thinking more along the lines of offensive driving," I said, making sure the straps around me were tight. "I realize we are on a timetable, but it would serve no one if we arrive in a flaming Tank, burnt to a crisp."

"O, ye of little faith," she said with a small laugh as she patted the dash of the car. "Cecil would be absolutely distressed to hear you speak ill of his craftsmanship. The Tank lives up to her name."

"Her?" I protested. "The Tank is not a her, the tank is most definitely masculine."

"Wrong," she said, cutting off another taxi. "She has a wide ass and an ample bosom. She's built for cruising, doing damage, and she always dishes out more than she receives. The Tank is a heartbreaker and a widowmaker. She has sweet curves, fine lines, and always looks good. The Tank is female —end of discussion."

"Well, when you put it that way, who am I to argue?"

"Exactly," she said. "Better call Grey and let him know we're on our way." She adjusted the rear-view mirror. "Tell him we may be bringing some unwanted friends."

"What?"

"Tails," she said, thumbing a finger behind her. "Three of them, unless you requested some escorts?"

"I requested no such thing," I said, turning around to observe three vehicles behind us. "You're not going to outrun them."

"Wasn't planning on it," she said, pulling the wheel hard to the left. "Those things are built for speed. Let's see how they handle some dancing."

"Dancing?" I said. "What are you—no."

"Oh yes, I call this dance the bump and grind," she said, accelerating down Park Avenue. "First, I need to see how determined they are."

The three black vehicles, which looked like modified Dodge Chargers, increased their speed to keep pace with us.

"They're driving Hellcats," she said as the smile returned to her face. "6.2-liter Hemi V-8's. Plenty of power, a shame it's housed in a delicate carbon fiber shell."

She slammed on the brakes, bringing the Tank to a sudden stop and let the lead Charger ram into our rear.

The entire front of the vehicle was crushed as she stepped on the gas and sped away with the remaining two vehicles in pursuit. The impact barely registered on the Tank. Several of the orange runes in the rear of the vehicle flared to life, but other than that, all I felt was a minor shudder.

I turned to look back and saw that the lead Charger was totaled, with smoke and steam billowing from the engine. The entire front of the car was a mangled mess. The carbon fiber may have made them faster, but it did nothing for their durability in withstanding an impact with the Tank. It was clear that these vehicles were not SuNaTran modified.

"They just don't make them like they used to," Tiger said with a chuckle. "One down, two to go."

"If they're Maledicta, they'll have more than two vehicles left to continue the chase," I said, looking behind and around us for more pursuers. "We need to lose them, or at the very least deter them from following us."

"Park Avenue is going to get crowded at the Helmsley Building," she said. "Grey is on the Lower East Side. I can head over to the FDR South to get them away from the populated center."

"Do it," I said as I dialed Grey. "Take them below Grand Central, then head east on 23rd Street. 23rd leads right into the FDR. That should be a less populated route—we want zero collateral. Property damage is one thing, loss of life due to reckless driving will bring all the authorities knocking on our door, starting with the NYTF."

"Got it," she said and swerved to the left again, racing down Park Avenue as the Met Life building could be seen in the distance. "Make sure your straps are secure. This is where we grind."

EIGHTEEN

I tightened the straps as the call connected with Grey.

"About time," he said with a growl. "I'm not getting any younger here. What did you do? Stop for a spot of tea with some biscuits?"

"First, I don't drink tea, I drink coffee as black as your soul," I said. "Second, we have a situation." I put the call through the Tank's audio system with a press of a button on the dash. "We have tails."

"How many and what kind?" he said. "Is this Maledicta?"

"I have every reason to believe so," I said. "Though I don't know what the instructions are...it makes no sense."

"It doesn't need to make sense," Grey said. "Heavy or light?"

"Lightweights but rockets, built for speed," Tiger answered as she swerved from lane to lane, barely avoiding the other vehicles around us. "Hellcat Chargers, carbon fiber, V-8s."

"Damn, this is not good," he said. "I have it on good information that I'm about to get violent, scaly guests—the dragon kind."

"We're on our way," I said. "Would they attack in your establishment? Isn't the Dive a de facto neutral zone?"

"Dragons have a tendency to believe that most rules don't apply to them," he said. "They only respect one law."

"The law of greater force," Tiger said. "Can you keep them civil until we get there?"

"I can be convincing when I need to be," he answered. "That doesn't mean *take forever*, though."

"I'm going to have to get creative with our escorts—there's no way I'm outrunning them."

"You're not supposed to," Grey said. "They're there to ride your rear and keep an eye on you. Have you removed any of them?"

"Took one of the three out," Tiger said with a smile. "Totaled it with the Tank. They're about as strong as wet toilet paper."

"Good job," he said with a small chuckle, making me question both their sanity. "I think it's safe to say Cecil didn't have a hand in upgrading them. Where are you headed?"

"FDR," she said. "Going to give them a surprise and it's going to make a bit of noise."

"How much noise?" he asked. "NYTF volume, or all the Councils and assorted authorities kind of volume?"

"Somewhere in between?"

He groaned in response.

"One second," he said with a growl, "I need my coffee."

"Any idea why they're pursuing us?" I asked. "Outside the usual 'they're trying to kill us', I mean."

"It's a funnel move," Grey said. "Light, fast cars will try and direct your route. More importantly, they will keep you in sight until the heavy hitters arrive on the scene. Have they opened fire yet?"

"Not yet," Tiger said. "I'm taking them on the scenic route to the FDR and then heading down to you."

"They're going to expect you hitting one of the highways, either the Westside or the FDR," he answered. "If you take them on the FDR, you're going to have to convince them to stop following you. Can you do it?"

"I have an idea," she said as we drove under the Helmsley building and onto the winding road that let us out on Park Avenue South. "It's going to be dicey, but I think I can pull it off."

"Do not alert the *entire* city," he said. "Trust me on this."

"I'll do my best to remain low-key," she said. "I'll make it so they take the heat. Will that work?"

"How many murdered out 66 Lincolns are in the city?" he asked. "That are associated with the Directive?"

"One," I said. "You're saying that whatever we do, they'll call us eventually?"

"Exactly," he said. "Be preemptive, call DAMNED and give the NYTF a heads-up—in that order, *before* you do whatever it is you're going to do. I'll get the garage ready. Your Tank is going to be hot for a few days after this. At least until we put out the fires with the NYTF and the DAMNED."

"Any other advice?"

"As much as possible, you want to limit the collateral to zero," he said, and I smiled. "I repeat: the *last* thing we need is the Councils on us."

"Really? I hadn't realized it would be a bad idea to go around mowing people down with our enormous murdered out 66 Lincoln," Tiger snapped. "Any other sage wisdom you two want to share with me while I try to avoid mage assassins?"

"Yes," he said. "Stop being a smartass and look out for the heavy vehicles."

"What kind?" I asked. "The Tank is formidable in its own right. I can't imagine many vehicles that can do it damage."

"Her," Tiger corrected. "Do *her* damage."

"Her," I stood corrected. "Not many vehicles can contend with her indestructibility. Cecil outdid himself with her."

"Keep an eye out for trucks, especially the armored kind," Grey said. "Those can pack a punch without having to be outfitted by Cecil. They don't need to destroy the Tank—actually, I doubt they can they just need to drive you into a wall or off a bridge. The point is to neutralize you, not blow you up, although I'm pretty sure they wouldn't mind that outcome."

"Neutralize us?" I said incredulously. "You do realize this vehicle has been dubbed the *Tank*?"

"If they manage to flip you over or drive you into the river, the name won't matter much, will it?"

"You have a point," I said, realizing the validity of his words. "What do we do with the light vehicles?"

"Remove them from the equation. They're a ploy to get you to run...right into their heavy hitters. Do *not* let them dictate the route you take, and get down here ASAP. By then, you should have the heavy escort. Don't get dead and avoid populated areas. Do I need to emphasize that speed would be good here?"

"No need," I said. "We will make haste."

"See that you do," he said. "Tiger?"

"Yes?"

"However fast you're driving right now, drive faster."

"Right away, dad," Tiger snapped and ended the call. "He sounds just like you."

"If you mean he sounds venerable and wise, then yes, I agree," I said. "He sounds very much like me."

"No, I meant annoying and cantankerous," she said. "How does he even know they're going to use heavy—"

A shadow in the night raced into us with a roar.

A black armored truck slammed into the side of the Tank

at that moment, ending Tiger's sentence. It shoved the Tank over and then overtook us.

"Bloody hell," I said as the impact sent us bouncing off several parked cars. "You were saying?"

Behind us, the Hellcat Chargers fell back and made room for another black armored truck to slide into position, blocking our rear.

We were trapped between them.

"Slash me sideways," she said "That thing actually moved the Tank."

"I noticed," I said as the armored truck behind us accelerated to keep pace. "That's no regular armored truck. There's no way it should be able to move at that speed."

"You think?" she said, flooring the gas pedal and shooting forward as she rode the rear of the truck in front of us. "It's been modified, and I lost eyes on the Chargers."

I looked around and saw that the two Chargers were no longer behind us. I took that as a bad sign.

"I don't see them," I said. "Stick to the route. Take them on the FDR and try to lose them there."

"If they think I'm going to make this easy for them, they have another thing coming," she said, gritting her teeth as she made a hard left onto 23rd Street. "They're going to regret chasing us today."

As she dodged traffic, she flipped the cover on the switch that would accelerate the Tank past the point of all reason.

NINETEEN

"I'm not certain this is the ideal location for us at the moment," I said, looking behind us as the rear truck bumped into the Tank. "They can easily try to crush—"

"We're not playing their game," she said, gripping the wheel hard. "Hold on, we're leaving this party."

She swerved the Tank into oncoming traffic, escaping the armored truck sandwich, right before the lead truck braked hard, its tires squealing as it came to a sudden stop. The rear truck was forced to brake suddenly to avoid smashing into the lead truck.

They had tried to crush us and failed.

"As if," she scoffed without so much as a glance behind us. "This isn't my first rodeo, you idiots."

She swerved back into the proper lane and shot down 23rd Street, heading east with both armored trucks in pursuit. They didn't lose much ground, remaining fairly close as their engines roared behind us. This only reinforced the thought that while they may not have been SuNaTran vehicles, whatever engines they were using were specifically designed to enhance their speed and maneuverability.

I saw the sign directing us to the FDR south, which was where we wanted to go. The Dive was located downtown from our current position. I saw her slow down and veer toward the entrance that led south.

"Why are you slowing down?" I asked. "I thought the point of outrunning a pursuer was to evade them?"

"I need them to commit," she said as she glanced into the rear-view mirror. "I'm dangling bait."

"Bait?" I asked, perplexed. "I thought we were the bait?"

"We're the ones doing the fishing now," she said, flooring the gas pedal and shooting forward through a red light. We nearly broadsided a small passenger vehicle that darted in front of us. The petrified face of the driver stared at us in abject terror as we bore down on him, only to miss by a hair's breadth from obliterating the vehicle into its component parts. I had no doubt that a collision between us would have resulted in the compact car being disintegrated upon impact, along with the driver, while the Tank would have remained unscathed. "That was close."

"That was close?" I said, raising my voice. There may have been a slight touch of hysteria in my voice. In my defense, we had just avoided sending some innocent stranger to an early grave by vehicular obliteration. "That was not close, that was absolute madness!"

"Listen, you really need to calm down," she said, without looking in my direction, while pulling a hard left and heading onto the FDR north service roadway. "Because if *that* freaked you out, you're *really* not going to like our next move."

"Our *next* move?" I asked as I read the signs. "I wasn't a fan of most of the previous moves. Why are you heading north? Grey is south from here."

"I know," she said with a small smile. "I told you, you wouldn't like our next move."

She sped onto the FDR heading north for several seconds, before cutting the driver's wheel hard to the left as she yanked the handbrake. It was a testament to Cecil's mechanical prowess and craftsmanship that the Tank responded as if it were a much smaller and incredibly nimble car, not a large boat of a vehicle.

We executed a 180, and ended up facing the oncoming traffic as Tiger released the brake and floored the gas. We were now heading south on the northbound roadway, which meant we were dodging vehicles every few seconds at high velocity.

If I didn't trust Tiger's driving skill implicitly, I would have forced her to stop the Tank before she smashed into some unsuspecting driver. I was *tempted* to stop her regardless, but I didn't.

For two reasons.

First, she was one of the best drivers I knew, and I knew some phenomenal drivers. Second, the armored trucks had mimicked Tiger's maneuver and had followed us onto the FDR, going south on the northbound roadway.

It would be an utter nightmare to keep track of the fast-moving black Tank in the night on a highway. They would have to contend with following us and dodging oncoming traffic.

"This is the opposite of keeping a low profile," I said. "Whoever is driving those trucks, they're insane to follow you. We'll have the NYTF on us in minutes."

"Maledicta probably frowns violently on failure to fulfill a mission," she said as she deftly weaved around the traffic. "Somehow, I don't see Regina doling out the punishments to a group of assassins."

"Nor do I," I said, holding onto the dash with a death grip as a couple of vehicles headed our way at speed. "The punishment department sounds like it may be delegated to Mura the Mountain."

"Makes sense."

I pressed my foot down on the imaginary brake pedal that failed to exist on my side of the Tank as I winced at the sight of cars coming at us.

"This is just a suggestion, mind you, but you may want to avoid them."

"No one likes a backseat driver, you know," she said, her focus completely on the cars heading our way and the road. "This is going to be tight, prepare for a pucker factor of ten."

"A pucker factor what—?"

Tiger accelerated the Tank in what appeared to be a suicidal ramming move, slid to the right to dodge one car, and then immediately swerved to the left while decreasing our velocity to dodge the second car.

She narrowly missed both cars, and...I understood what she meant by pucker factor.

If we were having difficulty avoiding traffic, it was exponentially worse for the armored trucks. They were forced to slow down as they pursued us, giving us time to formulate a plan. My current plan was retrieving my heart, which I had left abandoned on the FDR behind us, right after I regained my sanity and found a way to exit the Tank—alive.

"Bloody hell," I said. "Was that necessary?"

"Only if we want to stay alive and away from those two behind us," she said, picking up speed and glancing in the mirror. "Do you have eyes on them?"

"Yes, the grill on the lead truck is glowing," I said. "It seems they have activated some kind of runic attack."

She glanced quickly into the rear-view mirror.

"Seb, their grills are glowing orange," she pointed out, repeating what I had just said. "Why are their grills glowing?"

"I doubt it's for anything good," I said, rapidly turning around and looking behind us again. "Damnation."

Now the grills of both armored trucks were glowing a dull orange.

I focused on the trucks and partially used my sight. I saw the obscure runework covering the trucks. I couldn't read it, but I didn't need to.

I was fairly certain the symbols inscribed on the front of both trucks were simple to decipher—they probably meant something simple like 'pulverize anything you make contact with'.

"That can't be good," I said. "I strongly advise we avoid getting hit by those trucks, and by we, I mean you."

"Deduce that all on your own, did you?" she snapped. "Can you make out what the runes are for?"

"Do you really need a translation?" I snapped back. "I would think their purpose is clear. 'Destroy anything you ram' is my best guess."

"You're right, sorry," she said. "A translation isn't needed. We need to slow them down—more than this traffic is doing. You think they would cooperate and stop to let me cast a shield?"

"Of course," I said. "I'm certain they would oblige your request, right after they run you over and flatten you into paste. Have you gone mad?"

She laughed in response.

My phone which was still linked to the Tank rang.

I connected the call.

"This is not a good time," I said. "A little busy trying not to die in a flaming vehicular coffin."

"NYTF has mobilized several units and is headed your way," Rat said. "Traffic should be diminished, as they have closed off the FDR between 42nd Street and the Brooklyn Bridge."

I looked around and realized the traffic was getting light to non-existent. This was fast becoming a nightmare.

"To close that much of the FDR would require more than the NYTF," I said. "Who else is involved?"

"Apparently, the NYTF possesses more clout than we give them credit for," Rat replied as I heard the tapping of keys. "As of fifteen seconds ago, the only agency involved in this operation is the NYTF. However, DAMNED and the Light Council are being advised of events of importance as they occur."

'Events of importance' referred to anything that could be construed as supernatural. It was disguised in operational speech so as not to alarm any of the normals employed in the NYTF.

"Call me the moment any other agency gets involved," I said. "Do they have the Tank ID'd?"

"Not yet, but that won't last," he said. "You need to get hidden, fast."

"Understood," I said. "Keep me in the loop."

"Will do," he said and ended the call.

"Get ready," Tiger said. "We need to get off this merry-go-round, post haste."

"Get ready for what?"

"We're coming up to a straightaway," she said, looking ahead and pointing. "After that, it's the next exit and then Grey's place. We need to be off the FDR by then, or we'll run into our NYTF welcoming committee at the Brooklyn Bridge."

"That would be the worst of outcomes."

"Which is why we're getting off early," she said. "We'll use the exit."

"The exit that's on the other side of the FDR and across a concrete divider," I said, looking out and ahead of us. "How do you propose we do that? As far as I know, the Tank does not possess flight capabilities."

"It's good you can keep your sense of humor in moments like this," she said, dodging another few vehicles. "I'm going to need you to take the wheel as I create a kinetic net to stop them."

"A kinetic net?" I asked. "That won't be enough at this velocity. Those trucks have too much momentum and mass. Can you cast that while driving?"

"Right now, it's the best I have," she said, giving me a look. "I'm open to any ideas."

"I have some," I said. "I just thought you would possess something a little more robust in your kinetic arsenal, something with more stopping power."

She gave me a stare designed to maim, and then let out a long breath. I had the distinct impression she was counting to five in order to avoid stabbing me with one of her claws.

"I have *plenty* of stopping power, starting with my fists and claws," she said with a growl. "*You* want zero collateral, so I have to use something with more finesse, while I dodge traffic, avoid those two beasts behind us, *and* cast the kinetic net, which requires line of sight, all at the same time."

"Sounds doable. I think you can you handle it, I'll assist."

"Piece of cake," she answered through gritted teeth. "I don't know why I thought that would be complicated."

"Point made and taken. What do you want me to do as you unleash this kinetic net?" I asked, not being entirely familiar with the inner workings of kinetic nets. "What *exactly* are you going to do again?"

"No time to explain," she said, pulling the handbrake again as she yanked the wheel sharply to the right. She spun the Tank around without losing momentum, and we continued racing down the FDR, except now we were going south on the northbound road—in reverse. "Take the wheel and keep us from crashing!"

We were facing the angry, orange grills of the armored trucks as they picked up speed in an effort to impact the Tank. She floored the gas again, as she stuck half her body out of the driver's side window.

I grabbed the wheel and did my best to keep us from hitting the cars behind us as she gestured.

"Cast the strongest net you can," I said, gripping the wheel while looking behind us and avoiding oncoming traffic. "Make it fast."

"I need to see the target for these casts," she said, focusing. "Kinetic nets are timed casts with an explosive runic payload. The timing...the timing won't be as precise as I would like, but that can't be helped, given the circumstances."

"Explosive runic payload? "I asked, concerned. "How strong is the explosive component?"

"Not strong enough," she said, shooting me a glare. "It would be great if you could hold us still."

I ignored her glare.

"Doing my best, I'm not exactly an expert at driving in reverse on the highway while being pursued by angry assassins."

"Straightaway coming up," she said, her voice tight. "You do remember when I said this cast requires finesse?"

"I do," I said, swerving to avoid traffic. "The other drivers are being uncooperative."

"Keep us steady, and I might be able to pull this off."

"And if you don't?"

"If I screw this up, we are going to get very intimate with those orange grills in the next few seconds," she said, casting rapidly. "Like I said, keep us steady, so I can focus."

I steadied the Tank as we sped down the FDR.

"You are insane," I said as she unleashed a barrage of

semi-transparent orbs of energy at the armored trucks. The orbs attached themselves to the exteriors and pulsed with the same orange light as the grills. She quickly contorted her body to the front and cast a large shield designed to divert oncoming traffic away from the armored trucks. "How long before detonation?"

She twisted back into the driver's seat and took hold of the wheel as her large shield, which now looked like a concrete barrier, formed. It forced the oncoming traffic to our left.

"Two minutes, give or take," she said, glancing into the rear-view mirror. "Brace yourself."

"Brace myself? For what?"

"We need to turn around. The exit off the FDR, as you pointed out earlier, is on the opposite side," she said. "Hang on."

"Is that barrier going to work?" I asked, pointing at her cast. "Will it hold up to a collision?"

"It should, but there's only one way to find out," she said as she gracefully spun the Tank around to continue speeding downtown the wrong way. "Keep an eye on the trucks—the first set of orbs will weaken them, and the last set should slow them down, but it won't—"

"Stop them completely?" I finished. "Right?"

"They're going too fast to be stopped without a major explosion," she said. "Major explosion means major carnage in this neighborhood."

"Understood," I said. "I'll see what I can do."

She nodded silently as I contemplated our impending death.

She kept dodging traffic as we veered to the right, next to the concrete divider which separated the flow of north and southbound traffic on the FDR. We raced past the green highway sign as we headed for the upcoming exit.

The sign read Exit 5 Houston St. 1/2 MILE.

"I promise to get you fixed as soon as possible, baby," she said under her breath as she patted the dash. "I'm sure Cecil will understand. Just stay in one piece and get us through this."

"What are you doing?" I asked. "Are you *speaking* to the Tank?"

"Of course," she answered as if it was the most normal thing. "We need to do some demolition. I was just preparing her. Hold on."

She veered hard left for several seconds and then, without slowing down, cut a sharp right and...headed straight for the divider.

Holding the wheel straight, she smashed through the Jersey Barrier in the center of the FDR, leaving a Tank-sized hole in it, and obliterating the concrete that formed the divider.

I marveled at Cecil's skill in protective runework. We plowed through the concrete as if it wasn't there.

Any other vehicle would have hit that barrier and been demolished. As it impacted, the interior of the Tank erupted in orange runework as a cocoon of orange energy encased the Tank, protecting both herself and us.

I shuddered to think what the front of the Tank would look like after smashing through concrete like that, but I doubted the damage would be extensive—this was a SuNa-Tran vehicle after all.

By this point, we were mostly alone on the FDR, but I knew that this was due to the NYTF's closure of the FDR. It was only a matter of time before the units they dispatched caught up to us.

They had unknowingly given us all of the room we needed.

Now all we had to concern ourselves with were the trucks

giving chase. They swerved around what little remained of the oncoming traffic as we crossed over to the southbound side.

Moments later, the trucks crossed over to the southbound side also.

TWENTY

The armored trucks had plowed through the barrier, using the breach made by the Tank, sideswiping some straggling vehicles as they closed on us.

Whatever they had as engines, apparently had some kind of advanced turbo function. They were closing the gap between us with alarming speed.

"Tiger," I said, keeping my eyes on the trucks. "They're gaining."

"I'm going to slow down and take them off the FDR to the service roadway," she said, making no sense. "It's usually empty at this time, and the nets can detonate safely on that road without causing collateral damage."

"You're going to slow down?" I said, focusing on the trucks as I worked though the stasis darkcast in my head. "That can actually work, yes."

"Didn't you hear anything else I said?"

"I stopped paying attention after you said the words 'slow down'."

She shook her head.

"We need to let them think they have us," she said, "at least until the net detonates. Once we stop them, we'll go have a chat with our designated victims in those trucks. You do have a plan on how to stop them?"

"Something like that."

"This plan of yours is filling me with all sorts of confidence."

"It will work, I think," I said. "Can't you detonate those nets now?"

"I could, and they would impact all the vehicles around the trucks, including us," she said. "We're still too close—a detonation at this range would mean extensive collateral damage. So far we've kept that to a minimum. Do you want that to change?"

"Not in the least," I said. "Execute your plan."

She slowed the Tank and allowed the trucks to close the gap. The exit was on our right. She swerved onto it, pulling the trucks with her.

She was spot-on. Even in the early evening, the service road was empty of traffic and pedestrians. In the distance, I could hear sirens behind us.

So much for keeping this maneuver low-key.

My phone rang as she extended a hand out of her window and gestured. I put the call through, and Grey's voice growled through the Tank.

"NYTF is headed your way," he said. "Get to the Dive —now."

"Hold your horses, old man," Tiger said. "We're dealing with our escort."

"Where are you?" he asked. "How far out?"

"FDR just off the Houston Street exit, minutes away," she answered. "We'll be right there and we'll be coming in hot."

"Why would I expect anything less?"

He hung up as Tiger slowed the Tank down and rolled down the street as the armored trucks raced at us.

"This is going to be close," she said. I hope this doesn't break her."

"Shouldn't we be going faster than this though?"

"Yes, but any faster, we'll run out of road," she said continuing to gesture. "I'm going to need that extra road to escape the net and get us clear of the detonation."

She glanced ahead of us and flexed the muscles in her jaw. Putting the Tank in neutral she revved the engine, pushing it as we coasted. As the armored trucks approached, Tiger finished her gesture, detonating the kinetic net.

A lattice of orange tendrils erupted from the orbs on the trucks, attempting to root them in place. She threw the Tank in gear and flipped the switch at the same time.

The trucks were still going too fast, tearing up the street and pulling the kinetic net with them as they closed on us.

The Tank's hydraulics hissed as the chassis lowered to a few inches above street level, and the turbocharger kicked in, unleashing a piercing, earsplitting whine. That was drowned out a second later by the roar of the engine as we shot forward, racing away from the expanding kinetic net.

Thick tendrils of energy punched into the street behind us, disappearing into the asphalt as we sped away. I leaned out the passenger side window and gestured, unleashing the stasis darkcast.

Black energy erupted from my hands, joining the kinetic net in moments, as it clouded the edges of my vision. I felt the power I released merge and reinforce the orange tendrils around the trucks.

The kinetic net continued shooting tendrils into the street around us. More of its orange tendrils mixed with the stasis darkcast's energy punched into the trucks, robbing them of speed.

After a few seconds, the reinforced kinetic net stopped the trucks. As the Tank screeched to a stop, Tiger turned and stared at me.

"What was that?" she demanded. "What was that black energy?"

"Assistance," I said. "The stasis darkcast."

"You used the *darkcast*?" she asked, raising her voice. "Are you insane?"

"I didn't see another option," I said. "We needed to stop them."

She shook her head as she kicked open the door.

"That's how it starts," she said, pointing at me. "One justification at a time. Before you know it, you've gone full-blown darkmage."

"It needed to be done," I said, my tone ending all conversation. "You know I'm right."

"Being right doesn't make it right."

"Coming?" she asked as she set a foot outside. "We don't have all night. NYTF will be here soon."

"Let's go," I said and jumped out of the Tank, heading to the armored trucks. "I want to see who the bloody hell was—"

I was frozen in my tracks and pulled violently as Tiger grabbed me and threw me to the side. Simultaneously, she threw up a kinetic shield that took the brunt of the blast as both armored trucks exploded, launching us back several feet.

"I...I barely got that shield up in time," she said, shaken as we got to our feet. "Maledicta really doesn't take failure well, does it?"

"We need to be gone when the NYTF arrives," I said, heading back to the Tank. "There's nothing more for us to see here. Let's get the Tank off the street."

We jumped back in and turned right onto Houston Street.

Grey's building was located on 4th Street between Avenues C and D in a neighborhood called Alphabet City for obvious reasons.

It was once a rundown and dangerous neighborhood, but had like many neighborhoods in the city been an experiment of gentrification. Somehow, the building which housed the Dive had avoided the wave of renovations.

The three story building was an old carriage house Grey had converted into his home and business. The Dive itself was on the ground floor, and his home occupied the upper two floors.

The entire building was covered in extensive runework that deterred any kind of attack or surveillance. It was rumored that Grey owned not only the building, but the entire block.

"Doesn't the NYTF know about the Dive?" she asked as we headed down Houston Street. "Won't they come looking?"

"The Dive is a shadow neutral zone," I said. "The NYTF and even the Councils make it a point to avoid visiting Grey. Think of it as a mini-Switzerland in the city. No one brings violence to the Dive, unless they want it returned tenfold."

"I like his principles," she said, turning onto 4th Street. "Can they track us?"

"They have no reason to suspect us yet," I said, pointing at the open garage on the ground floor of the converted carriage house. "There, take us in there."

Tiger crushed the brakes and turned us sideways, drifting the Tank into the space with little room to spare.

Grey who was standing outside, gave her a nod of satisfaction and proceeded to close the garage door. I felt the presence of the dampening runes come to life as the door closed.

Every surface bore runes, creating a magical vacuum. In order to cast in the Dive, it would require staggering amounts of magical energy, which would only be met with lethal fail-safes if attempted.

We were safe...for now.

TWENTY-ONE

We stepped out of the Tank and headed toward the Dive proper.

Tiger brought up the rear after she examined the Tank and not so surprisingly found little damage to its front.

It was dubbed the Tank for a reason.

"I can't believe it survived breaking through that concrete barrier," she said as we stepped into the Dive. "That would have totaled any other car."

The runes on the door hummed with latent power as we entered. "I know a few other cars that would have survived that maneuver," I said as Grey stepped into the space. "His Beast for one." I turned to Grey who approached us. "I didn't see it outside—has Cecil finally put it out of its misery?"

"The Beast can't die," Grey said. "She is indestructible and parked across town at the Abyss."

"The Abyss?" Tiger asked as we headed to the bar, where I smelled a fresh pot of coffee brewing. "What's the Abyss?"

"Later," Grey said as he stepped behind the bar. "Did the NYTF ID you?"

"No," I said. "We managed to leave the scene before they showed up."

"Good," he said, pouring himself a large mug of coffee. "Death Wish?"

"Two, please," I said, after glancing at Tiger who nodded. "You've renovated the place."

"Some," he said. "Redid some of the runes and added others. We've had a few incidents due to your cousin and his associate. I swear, between those two and Strong's hellhound, I'm surprised any buildings are still standing in the city."

"They do have some...destructive tendencies," I said, taking the offered mug he placed in front of me. I turned to admire the interior as I took a sip. "This is good."

He nodded in agreement as he took a long pull from his steaming mug. The interior of the Dive had retained its old world charm. It was a mixture of mahogany and cherry woods. The bar appeared to be carved out of one large piece of runically enhanced wood.

In fact, like the garage, every surface was covered in runes, continuing the magical vacuum. It would be nearly impossible to cast in here as well.

I let my sight expand and noticed the state-of-the-art security system embedded into the walls, floor, and ceiling. Grey may have been a seasoned mage, but he wasn't a stranger to cutting-edge technology and apparently utilized it to his benefit.

The aroma of the coffee filled the bar-restaurant, but I noticed it was devoid of patrons and staff. Over the speakers, the smooth voice of Daniel Castro was inviting me over to listen to him play the blues.

"Castro?" I said as the music continued. "This track is quite apropos."

Grey raised an eyebrow at me and nodded, lifting his mug.

"You know your music," he said, closing his eyes as a guitar wailed in the background. "It's a solid track."

I nodded.

Tiger drank from her mug and nodded.

"This place is a magical null space," she said. "How did you manage that?"

"Many runes and many years," Grey said as he glanced at the door. "Wasn't easy and requires constant upkeep."

I looked around the Dive.

For a neutral zone, even an informal one, I didn't expect it to be this deserted.

"Where is everyone?" I asked. "Aren't all neutral zones supposed to be open twenty-four hours a day?"

"Staff is across town today," he said. "Except for Frank who's floating around somewhere doing who knows what, and one chef to prepare some light meals. You're right though, neutral zones are open twenty-four seven. The official ones."

"Which the Dive is not," I said. "So, you're allowed to have off hours."

"This is still a business with regular customers," he answered. "We still maintain close to twenty-four seven—probably closer to twenty-four six—but if someone's in a pinch and needs sanctuary, the Dive is always open."

"You were saying something about guests?" I asked after taking a pull from my mug. "Of the scaled persuasion?"

"Word on the street is that Maledicta has gone rogue," he said. "Issued an open challenge to Cynder and her Wyverns."

"Shit," Tiger said. "That's suicide. Has Regina lost her mind?"

"Possibly," Grey said. "Cynder can't let this challenge go unanswered. Loss of face and all that nonsense. Bottom line? Maledicta going rogue is bad for business."

"What does that have to do with you?" I asked. "You're not part of Maledicta."

"Cynder contacted me to deal with Regina and Maledicta," he said. "She's going to want to know why this is still an active issue."

"Meaning?"

"You know what that means—do I need to spell it out for you?"

"I do, but I want to hear you say it," I said. "Just so we're on the same page."

"I didn't have to contact you, Eyes," Grey said. "You don't want to go down this path, we're on the same side in this. I'm not your enemy."

"Nor I yours, but I want to make sure we're clear here, no ambiguity," I said. "When the time comes, I and the Directive will deal with Regina, and you will deal with Maledicta."

"Who's going to deal with Cynder and her dragons?" Tiger asked. "Sooner or later, we're going to have to face off against them."

"I wasn't aware we were going to war with them as well," Grey said. "If you want us to make *that* move, you're going to need more firepower than you currently have. I don't think that's a war you want. Are you willing to go to battle with Char?"

"No," Tiger said. "That would be unwise in any scenario."

"What do you think is going to happen if you attack Cynder, or worse somehow manage against the odds to punch her ticket and eliminate her?" Grey said. "You think Char is just going to look the other way? After you kill one of her own?"

"We're charkin," Tiger said, presenting the weakest of arguments. "She knows what happens in warfare—she's a dragon."

"Not only does she know, she will give you a firsthand demonstration of what happens when you truly anger an old dragon," he said. "One with ancient power. Want my advice?

We take out Maledicta, and you deal with Regina any way you see fit. Cynder will be upset, but she can't stop you."

"And Char?" Tiger asked "You don't think she's going to interfere?"

"As long as you leave Cynder out of the attack plans, Char will remain neutral," he said. "The moment you attack Cynder, you'll see how much those marks are worth, when she blasts you both from the face of the earth."

"Agreed," I said, glancing at Tiger. "Cynder is not an option. I know how much you want to face off against Beatrix, but unless it's sanctioned, we leave Cynder and all of the Wyvern alone. They are non-combatants."

"What if Beatrix attacks me?"

"I like how you think," Grey said with a grin as he shook his head. "Still suicide though. You're charkin and expected to behave in a manner respectful of your station. You both represent Char as her kin. Behaving in a manner that dishonors her can get you terminated."

"You're serious?" Tiger asked. "If we make her lose face, we can lose our lives?"

"Yes," Grey replied. "You're familiar with the whole samurai representing his daimyo concept? Any samurai who dishonored his lord could be ordered to commit *seppuku*—ritual suicide to restore honor. That was the norm and expected."

"Yes, I'm familiar with the practice," Tiger said. "What does that—?"

"Where do you think feudal Japan got the idea?" Grey said, interrupting her. "They borrowed it from an old clan of dragons. Over time, it spread all over the country."

"Fascinating," I said. "As much as I respect history, I have no intention of living out the last moments of a samurai. Cynder and her Wyvern are off-limits. Period."

Grey nodded and took another long pull from his mug.

"You can explain it to her when she gets here," he said, glancing at the entrance. "Shouldn't be too long now."

"How do you know she's going to pay you a visit," Tiger asked, following his gaze with her own. "She give you a copy of her schedule?"

"Funny," Grey said with a growl. "No, she summoned me to her palace in the sky."

"The Eyrie," I said. "Her base of operations."

"Her lair," Grey corrected. "What is it with dragons and their lairs? Anyway, I not-so-politely declined her invitation. I told her I don't make house calls."

"What did she say?" Tiger asked with small laugh. "I bet she was pissed."

"That'd be one way to put it, yes," Grey said. "She said, fortunately for me, she does."

"Then, a few of my sources informed me she left her building with two of her security—a large beast of a man with long hair, and a tall, dangerous-looking lady. I have to assume they're both dragons as well."

"You'd assume correctly," Tiger said. "That sounds like Alexander and Beatrix."

"Those were the names I was given," Grey said. "I'm figuring she should be here any minute, though she may have to take an alternate route since the FDR is closed this evening, due to some reckless driving."

Tiger smiled.

"I live for the small pleasures," she said. "What are you going to tell her?"

The frame around the threshold to the Dive blazed with orange and violet light as a knock could be heard on the door.

"I'm going to tell her to come in," Grey said. "I'm not in the mood to replace a runed, Australian Buloke door. It would be aggravating and expensive."

With a gesture, he unlocked the door and it opened,

becoming slightly ajar. The runes on and around the door went from vibrant violet to brilliant red.

"Come in," Grey said with another gesture, disabling the runes at the door. "I've been expecting you."

The door opened wider, and Cynder walked in, with Alexander and Beatrix joining her a few seconds later. She took a few steps forward and stared at Grey.

"I'm sure you have, Night Warden," Cynder said, stepping farther into the Dive. "We need to talk."

TWENTY-TWO

Cynder took a moment to scan the interior of the Dive.

She gave Tiger and me a cursory glance and continued surveying the rest of the bar-restaurant.

"Your establishment is...what do you call this decor?" she asked. "Marginally homeless?"

"Your privilege is showing," Grey said with a slight smile, dismissing the insult. "It suits me and my clientele just fine."

"This clientele of which you speak," Cynder said, still scanning the interior, "they actually pay for the opportunity to frequent this location? Of their own volition?"

"Feel free to take a seat," Grey said, motioning to the interior with a hand, as he remained behind the bar, sipping from his mug. "Wherever you feel comfortable works."

"Thank you, no," she said. "I feel *comfortable* in my Eyrie." She returned her gaze to Grey. "Why did you refuse my summons earlier this evening?"

"I don't work for you," Grey said, and I saw the muscles in Alexander's jaw twitch. Usually, he was fairly easy going, except when it came to Cynder. Most of the Wyvern were touchy when it came to their Lady. "I don't work for *anyone*."

"Do you realize stronger mages than you have died for less?" Cynder said with a smile. "To refuse a dragon of my stature is tantamount to suicide."

Grey took another long pull from his mug before answering. I marveled at his willingness to face death with such disregard.

"Really? I wasn't aware," Grey said with a smile that matched Cynder's. "I hope you didn't leave your sky-palace and travel all the way down here to grace me with your presence in my marginally homeless hovel, and to inform me how respected you are and how terrified I should be. You could have called and saved yourself a trip."

Alexander took a step forward.

"You dare?" Alexander said through gritted teeth. "Apologize."

"For?" Grey asked. "As far as I can tell, I'm the one who's been insulted."

"Apologize or I will be forced to take steps," Alexander warned. "Do it, now."

Grey put his mug down on the bar and leaned back, taking in the immensity that was Alexander, before turning his gaze to Cynder. Beatrix remained still and silent by Cynder's side and stared at Tiger and me.

"I feel it's only fair to warn you before you take your *steps*," Grey said, keeping his voice calm and placing an enormous hand cannon on the bar. "I think it's the polite and right thing to do."

He looked at Cynder and nodded. She returned the nod.

"Is that *toy* supposed to frighten me?" Alexander said, looking at Grey with contempt. "Guns are meaningless against me and my kind."

"I figured as much, which is why I put it on the bar," Grey answered. "I have no intention of drawing Fatebringer on you."

"How quaint, you named your toy pistol," Alexander scoffed when he should have been paying attention. "Apologize, you old, broken-down excuse of a mage." He turned to Cynder. "Lady Cynder, why did you even dignify this cesspool of an establishment with your presence? Let me end this mage and we can leave this place now." He glanced disdainfully at Grey. "I doubt he can even cast."

The energy in the Dive had shifted from tense to an undercurrent of lethality. I knew the runes in the Dive were potent, but I didn't know if they were strong enough to deter not one but three dragons from attacking us.

Beatrix crossed her arms and took a step back to lean against the nearest wall. Cynder moved over to the bar and sat on one of the stools, turning to take in the scene playing out. Only Alexander stood in the center of the floor, demanding Grey apologize to his Lady.

I moved Tiger over to one side to make sure we were out of the line of fire and went to stand on the far end of the bar, ready to jump behind it for cover if need be.

"Oh, I can still cast," Grey said, keeping his voice light. "Are you sure you want to force me to apologize to your Lady?"

"You should be on your knees," Alexander said with a snarl. "I can break them for you and make it easier to kneel."

Grey stepped out from behind the bar. He was wearing a black T-shirt, jeans, and construction boots. I could understand how he could be misinterpreted for anything, but a powerful mage.

It would be an honest mistake, but it would still be a error. I was certain many of his enemies had underestimated him based on his appearance.

It was most likely their last miscalculation.

I looked around and saw his signature duster hanging from a hook near the bar. Looking at the runes that covered it, I marveled at the intricacy of the runework and the power in its signature.

The only thing that compared was Cecil's runework on his vehicles. From what I could decipher, Grey's duster was indestructible and possessed immense space, which felt wrong, somehow.

To my sight, it read as a portal, not a garment to be worn.

It appeared larger than it looked. I had to be mistaken and attributed the misread to the amount of runes inside the Dive throwing off my sight.

"Don't kill him, Warden, he is very good at his job and would be difficult to replace," Cynder said. "Perhaps a gentle check is in order."

"That's up to him," Grey said. "Let's see where this conversation goes."

"Very well," Cynder said with a slight nod. "Remember his age."

Grey nodded and approached Alexander, stopping about five feet away from the giant man. The disparity between the two was stark as Grey looked up to address Alexander.

"Lady Cynder?" Alexander said. "Surely you don't think this excuse of a mage can pose a threat to me?"

"We reap and we sow," she said with a wave of her hand. "I have pled for your life. The Night Warden is an honorable mage, he won't kill you, but he *may* hurt you."

Alexander unleashed a malicious grin in Grey's direction.

I shook my head and moved back, pulling Tiger with me. I wasn't completely sure of what was going on, but I did know a few things.

Grey had survived on the streets of this city, alone as the last Night Warden, for a very long time. The adage of being wary of an old man in a profession where men died young applied here.

It was no accident that Grey had survived this long.

He was cunning, devious, and most importantly, an expert tactician. He knew how to face overwhelming odds and emerge victorious.

I had the feeling that Alexander hadn't faced overwhelming odds a day in his long life. There was also the matter of the defenses in the Dive. I let my senses expand, feeling their runic power thrumming through the building. They were potent but currently dormant.

Grey had deactivated most of the overt failsafes and defenses when we arrived, but from what I could feel, he had an array of horrifically devastating deterrents only a thought away.

Then, there was Grey himself.

I had tried to get a read on him when we entered the Dive, and he came up a blank. Not because he lacked an energy signature, quite the opposite, he possessed so much power, that he read as white noise to my senses.

It was as if his power level was too high for me to register. I was fairly certain that was due to the sword he had bonded to, but I had no way of knowing for sure. There was also the matter of what *kind* of mage he was.

Grey was a darkmage.

It meant that his body of magical knowledge was not limited to utilitarian casts. He possessed knowledge considered banned and off-limits to most sect mages.

And there was one more clue that Alexander either chose to ignore or just missed completely. Cynder had *chosen* to come to the Dive, even *after* Grey refused to answer her summons.

She had come to him.

"This is not going to end well," Tiger said under her breath next to me. "Grey appears to be an old, tired mage, but most of that is an act. He has real power. If I had to guess...dragon-ending power."

I nodded.

I looked around and realized that if this turned into a real battle, the safest place we could be right now would be very far away.

We were standing in ground zero.

TWENTY-THREE

"Come then, old man," Alexander said. "I will help you kneel before my Lady."

"Are you sure you need him?" Grey said, without looking at Cynder. "You could always get someone else, someone with a working brain—or manners, at least."

"No, I prefer him," Cynder replied, glancing at Alexander. "He is loyal to a fault, as you can see, and he is one of my first Wyvern, along with Beatrix. It would be too difficult to replace him—not impossible of course—but I do not wish to go through that process again for at least a few centuries."

"You didn't brief him," Grey said. It wasn't a question. "You knew he would act this way."

"All of my Wyvern have a certain degree of bravado," she said. "We *are* dragons after all. The ego comes with the package, but every so often, it profits me to help them realize that the world is much larger than they imagine. Even dragons face threats, even dragons have limits."

Now I knew why Cynder had made the trip to the Dive— she was using this opportunity and Grey as a teachable moment for Alexander. That deviousness was what made her dangerous.

Grey reached over to the bar and grabbed his mug again.

"This is going to hurt like hell," he said before taking another pull. "Not you, me."

"You're finally coming to your senses," Alexander said with a nod. "Is it fear?"

"Nothing wrong with my senses," Grey said. "As for fear, I stopped feeling fear the day I lost my heart." He looked off to the side for a few moments, an expression of pain briefly crossing his face. "Nothing to fear after that. However, I have reconsidered confronting you directly, though. I *am* getting too old for ego contests that prove what I already know."

"You finally realize who you are facing, *what* you are facing," Alexander said with a smile. "Do your bones tremble, old man?"

"Okay," Grey said, putting down the mug. "Enough with the 'old man' nonsense."

He gestured, and all of the defenses of the Dive activated at once. The effect was immediate and overwhelming.

A wall of runic pressure descended, crushing us where we stood. Grey looked at me and pointed to a glowing circle on the floor next to where Tiger and I stood.

We stumbled over to stand in the circle, and the effects of the defenses lessened considerably. They didn't disappear completely, but I could breathe without feeling the weight of an elephant on my chest.

"What the hell was that?" Tiger asked as blood trickled from her nose and she pointed at me. "Slash me sideways, you're bleeding."

"So are you," I said as I removed some napkins from the bar, handed her one, and wiped the blood from my face. "He activated the Dive's defenses."

"You misunderstand," Grey continued, reaching over to

another stack of napkins and grabbing a few. He walked over to Beatrix and handed her one. She looked at him, surprised. He pointed to his face, then to hers. Then, he walked over to Alexander and raised a napkin to him. "You're going to need this."

I looked over at Beatrix and saw a trickle of blood escape slowly from her nose. Her eyes widened as she placed the napkin on her face.

"Shit," Beatrix said. "You did this?"

Grey nodded as he stepped over to Alexander.

Alexander glanced over at Beatrix, and I could see the anger rise in his face, taking over his thought process.

"You dare attack us?" he said. "That will cost you, mage."

Grey remained still and held out the napkin to him.

"Take it," Grey said. "You don't want to ruin that nice suit."

"What is that?" Alexander scoffed, glaring at the white napkin. "Are you signaling surrender? It's too late for that now, mage."

Alexander made to bat Grey's hand away with his own, and found that he couldn't. When his hand connected with Grey's, it remained immobile.

Shock and surprise replaced the anger in his expression.

Blood began to trickle down from Alexander's nose.

The only one who appeared unaffected, besides Grey, was Cynder. Upon closer inspection, I saw the muscles in her jaw flex, as she gripped the bar in a death grip. Her face remained calm. I realized that she *was* being affected, she was just better at dealing with the effects than her Wyvern.

"The loss of power and strength you're experiencing is level two of the Dive's defenses," Grey said, before taking another leisurely pull from his mug as he looked up into Alexander's shocked face. "Uncomfortable, isn't it? I recently upgraded to five levels. Mostly due to guests much stronger than you three. Since your Lady asked me not to kill you, and I'm in an obliging mood, I won't go above the third level. You're a misguided, arrogant ass, but you don't deserve that kind of agony."

"What have you done?" Alexander demanded. "*How?*"

Grey held up the napkin again and Alexander took it this time.

"I've deterred you from doing something foolish in a neutral zone and *my home*," Grey said, the last words carrying a dangerous edge. "How doesn't really matter, does it? This was a simple cast just to let you know I still can. Do you yield?"

"To you? Never," Alexander said in his continued lapse of self-preservation. "You are only a mage."

"I had a feeling you would say that." Grey glanced over at Cynder. "You do have an infirmary over in your sky-palace?"

"It's the Eyrie, and yes, we do," Cynder managed with some difficulty. "Should I notify them?"

Grey nodded.

"Yep," he said. "Tell them to prepare the extra-large bed for your dragon here. He's going to need it."

"You would attack me while disadvantaged?" Alexander said. "You are honorless."

"My honor is not a fragile thing," Grey said, his words hard, "and *you* are not worthy to pass judgment on it. You have not earned the right. I told you, I've reconsidered confronting you directly."

"Then what's this, a deception?"

"No, this is me, calling my head of security to deal with a perceived threat," Grey said, heading back behind the bar. "I'll even make it fair, so there are no excuses and no misunderstandings afterwards."

"You'll what?" Alexander demanded. "Make it fair how?"

Grey gestured and I felt the pressure in the Dive diminish. Cynder and Beatrix visibly relaxed, releasing the tension in their faces and bodies. Even Alexander's posture changed as strength flowed back into him.

A few moments later, the air became charged to the point that I felt the hairs on the back of my neck stand on end.

"That can't be good," Tiger said, watching small electrical arcs form on the surface of the bar. "What is that?"

"That," I said, "is trouble. Get your strongest deflective shield ready."

"My strongest deflective—?"

"Do it," I hissed. "Now."

She gestured and prepared a shield.

"I'm ready," she said. "What exactly am I ready *for*?"

"Nothing, I hope," I said. "We're just taking the necessary precautions in order to leave the Dive tonight—alive."

From the buildup of energy I sensed around us, I didn't know if it would be enough. I could only hope he didn't unleash a blast and inadvertently incinerate us in the process.

A spike in the energy caught my attention, and I moved us back to the farthest edge of the circle we stood in.

"What the fu—?" Tiger never managed to finish her sentence.

A lightning bolt descended into the Dive, crashing into the bar and filling the air with the smell of chlorine and burning wires. A loud thunderclap followed, rattling the bottles behind the bar.

Grey shook his head slightly, rolling his eyes at the lightning and thunder, and reached behind the bar for a medium-sized bar towel covered in intricate runes.

On the bar, in the midst of several small fires, stood an eight-inch thorny dragon turning slowly as he scanned the room.

"Do you recall earlier when I asked about a small, electrical lizard?" I asked. "That is who I was referring to."

"You had me prepare a shield for a tiny lizard?" she asked. "Are you serious? You have got to be kidding."

She moved to step out of the circle, and I grabbed her arm and shook my head.

"You know how you hate it when people underestimate you because you don't necessarily *appear* imposing?" I asked. "Then you proceed to dispel their assumptions by shredding said victim to pieces?"

"Yes," she warned. "What of it?"

"You're making the same mistake here," I said, pointing at the thorny dragon. "That is Frank and he is much more than he appears. Stay in the circle and keep that shield ready."

TWENTY-FOUR

Frank turned in a circle and then looked at Grey, before he spat on the bar, causing a small fire. Grey dropped the runed towel on the fire, putting it out immediately.

"Lightning *and* thunder?" Grey asked. "Really? You don't think that was a little much?"

"I've been practicing my entrance," Frank said, shaking his tail. "You went to level two. That deserves a special entrance. Why did you go to level two?" He scanned the interior of the Dive. "Where's the threat? I see three dragons—two of them still too young to be anything more than annoying—and two mages who barely register as a menace. Is that Cynder?"

"Hello, Francis," Cynder said, giving Frank a slight nod of recognition. "How have you been?"

"Hello, Cynder. Up until this moment, I've *been* enjoying a quiet afternoon on my day off," Frank said, glaring at Grey. "Then Grey, the last Warden relic, decides it's time to call me down here for a situation he can handle in his *sleep*."

"You're the head of security," Grey said with a growl. "I

need you to do some securing, since you barely do anything else around here, besides aggravate me."

"Seriously, you had me prep a shield for this?" Tiger said under her breath. "I could stomp on that lizard and end him."

"You could try," I said, keeping my voice low. "You would regret it almost instantly."

"I'm not seeing the menace," Tiger said. "He's tiny."

"Grey, you don't think this is overkill?" Cynder said. "There was no need to summon Francis."

"He'll behave. This way, I avoid casting," Grey said, "and a possible migraine."

"Oh, you just didn't want to handle *this*," Frank said. "Fine, why am I down here? Who needs to be secured? The mages or the dragon whelps?"

"There's no need to be all dramatic," Grey said, wiping down the bar and preventing other small fires from forming, as small arcs of energy jumped off Frank's body. Grey looked over the bar and motioned to Alexander with his mug. "Frank, that's Alexander. Alexander, this here is Frank, resident pain in my ass and the head of security for the Dive."

"*This* is your head of security?" Alexander scoffed. "You summoned this little creature to threaten me... This insignificant *lizard*?"

"I really wish you hadn't said that," Grey answered with a wince. "Frank is very much like my duster hanging over there."

"Where are you going with this, Grey?" Frank asked. "Your duster?"

"Yes," Grey said with a nod. "He appears small on the outside, but is exponentially larger inside. Frank is a dragon."

"That was pretty good, I approve," Frank said with a nod. "I see who needs securing. Do I melt him now?"

"No," Grey said. "No melting."

Alexander laughed and Beatrix raised an eyebrow as she stared from Grey to Frank and back to Grey again.

"A dragon!" Alexander said, raising his voice and pointing at Frank. "Now I know fear has addled your mind, old man. You call this *lizard* to confront me because you fear facing me yourself?"

"Alexander..." Beatrix warned. "Measure your words."

"Or else what?" Alexander scoffed. "The fearsome *dragon* will teach me a lesson? Oh, my apologies, I said dragon. I meant puny *lizard*."

Frank turned to Grey and shook his tail.

"For this?" Frank said, accusation in his voice. "You called me down here for this ignorance?"

"Figured you haven't fried a dragon in some time," Grey said before taking another pull from his mug. "This will let you work off some of that ever-present crankiness you call a temperament. Just don't kill him, Cynder likes the idiot."

Frank turned to Cynder who nodded in his direction.

"Fine, no killing," Frank said, throwing up one of his feet and turning to face Alexander. "What's your name, Tall-dark-and-braindead?"

"I am Alexander, first Wyvern of the Nine," he proclaimed. "We are the dragons who serve Lady Cynder."

"Quite a pedigree," Frank said with a nod. "Mine is not as impressive as yours, I'm sure."

"I don't doubt it," Alexander replied. "Who are you?"

"I am Francis, Archmagus of the Grand Sect of the Abyss, destroyed by my own hand when I attempted my final transmutation into a lesser being."

"Lesser being?" Alexander asked, still not picking up on the pertinent clues, like the words 'Archmagus' and 'Grand Sect of the Abyss', an infamous sect in history formed entirely of darkmages wielding unimaginable power, followed by the words, 'destroyed by my own hand'. "What lesser being?"

"That of a dragon," Frank said, shaking his tail slowly. "It could be I simply miscalculated—dragons are such simple creatures. I probably overcorrected for that simplicity and, well, here we are."

"Simple creatures?" Alexander said, offended. "I could crush you with a fist."

"And he goes on to prove my point," Frank said, glancing at Cynder. "Are you *certain* you want to keep him?"

"Quite," Cynder said. "Don't kill him."

Frank turned to Grey.

"I'm taking the next two days off," he said. "Get Cole to cover for me, unless you have more *securing* for me to do?"

"What kind of head of security takes days off," Grey said. "You're amazing."

"What I am...is angry and irritable," Frank said with a rapid tail shake. "Two days."

"Fine," Grey said, throwing up a hand. "I'll let Cole know. Deal with this. We have matters to discuss."

"Oh, now you're rushing me?" Frank muttered. "First, I don't do anything, and now, it's *hurry up and get it done*, you are incredible."

"Frank, I'm not getting any younger," Grey snapped. "I'm serious, we're on a tight schedule."

"Finally said something I can agree with—you are not getting any younger," Frank snapped. "You may want to activate the defenses to at least level three. Alex here is about to be enlightened."

"That's your warning?" Grey said, gesturing rapidly and bringing the defenses of the Dive back to their previous level and beyond. "Level three, really?"

"You wanted fast, precise, and powerful, but not lethal," Frank said. "I can only give you two in this short time frame."

"Which means?" Grey said, increasing the level of the defenses until it became difficult to think due to the flow of energy in the Dive. "There, done, level three."

"Which means precision has been sacrificed, slightly," Frank said, cocking his head to the side and looking up. "I wouldn't stand too close to Alex over there for the next three...two...now."

A bolt of blinding blue-white electrical energy punched into Alexander from above, enveloping him in a surge of power that I was certain would kill him where he stood.

As Alexander dealt with an instant microwaving, I saw Beatrix sag against the wall, barely managing to remain upright. Only Cynder seemed to deal with the increase in the defense level with little visible discomfort.

"The deflective shield. Cast it," I said as both Tiger and I averted our gaze from Alexander, who stood riveted in place, literally glowing as he was caught in the flow of power and helpless to do anything except suffer. "Cast it!"

Tiger cast her shield, surrounding us with kinetic energy.

"I hope that's strong enough," Tiger said, focused on Alexander. "Is he going to kill him?"

"I don't know," I said. "I've never felt this much concentrated electrical runic power in one location before. I'm surprised he's still alive."

"Dragons are tough, but I'm not sure even he can take this for much longer," Tiger said, reinforcing her shield. "Is he *trying* to kill him?"

"I think if Frank wanted to kill him, he wouldn't need to *try*."

Alexander was locked in place where he stood, his face frozen in a rictus of agony, as the energy coursed through and around his body. I saw his suit begin to smolder and catch flame. His hair disappeared in seconds, disintegrated from the blast.

"He was due for a haircut anyway," Frank said. "No one wears their hair long any more. Who does he think he is— Fabio? That's so twenty years ago."

"Francis," Cynder said, "I think he learned his lesson."

"A few more seconds and you'll have a vacancy in your ranks," Frank said, looking at the smoldering Alexander. "It's not too late to reconsider."

"No, thank you, Francis," Cynder said. "Please release him."

"Well, if you're going to be polite about it, how can I refuse?"

Frank nodded and said something under his breath I couldn't quite make out. The bolt of energy stopped immediately. Tiger dropped her shield moments later.

Alexander staggered in the middle of the Dive with a dazed expression on his face. After a few moments, his eyes rolled up into his head and he fell back, crashing onto the floor.

"Is he dead?" Beatrix asked, concerned. "Did you *kill* him?"

"No," Frank said. "But he's going to be hurting for a few weeks, and his hair is going to take some time to grow back. A nice reminder whenever he looks in the mirror not to be such an asshat."

"But he *will* live?" Cynder asked, looking at the smoking body of Alexander. "You're certain?"

"Unfortunately, yes," Frank said. "He will recover completely and maybe with some hard-earned humility." He turned to Grey. "Will that be all, Your Majesty? Or do you need someone else secured? I could barbecue the mages. Isn't the one in the glasses related to Montague?"

"No, I mean yes, he is related, but no, no more securing will be needed."

"You sure?" Frank asked. "He looks like he may be planning some mischief. Has he destroyed any buildings lately?"

"None. You don't plan on leaving the dragon there, do you?" Grey asked, pointing at Alexander. "He's blocking the middle of the floor."

"He's not *my* dragon," Frank said. "He belongs to Cynder. Ask her to move him."

"He belongs in an infirmary," Cynder said. "Francis, *you* charbroiled him."

"Well?" Grey said, crossing his arms and staring at Frank. "He can't stay in the middle of the Dive. He clashes with everything and I just had the floors done."

"Oh, hilarious," Frank said. "Are you suggesting *I* take him to an infirmary?"

"You broke him, you get to help fix him," Grey said, glancing at Cynder. "Cynder's infirmary in her sky-palace will be expecting him."

Cynder nodded.

"How soon can you get him there?" Cynder asked. "Alexander does need medical attention immediately. His healing will take some time to deal with the damage inflicted."

"If I teleport, a matter of seconds," Frank said. "*If* I teleport."

"Frank..." Grey said, his voice a barely veiled threat. "It's the least you can do, after that world-class barbecuing you gave him."

Cynder pulled out a phone, pressing a button and spoke low into it when the call connected. She ended the call a few seconds later.

"They are waiting for you now," she said. "I would consider it a personal favor if you would be so kind as to transport my Wyvern to the infirmary in the Eyrie, Francis."

Frank turned to Grey.

"See?" Frank said, pointing an arm at Cynder. "*That* is how you make a request. I still don't want to do it, but she asked nicely, so I will."

"I asked nicely," Grey said with a low growl. "Didn't I?"

"Ask? When did you ask?"

"Fine, I didn't ask," Grey admitted. "But I threatened nicely. Didn't you hear how I said your name? There was barely any menace in my voice."

"Hopeless," Frank said, jumping off the bar and skittering over to Alexander's body. "There's no fixing you, Grey. You are a lost cause."

"Tell me something I don't know," Grey said with a shrug. "See you in three days. You deserve the extra day for transportation."

"I hate you a little less now," Frank said, somewhat placated. "Unless the world is ending, I am not available and off the clock."

"Understood," Grey said. "Enjoy your time off."

"Cynder," Frank said with a bow. "He'll be fine. You may want to have a talk with him when he regains consciousness."

"Thank you," Cynder said. "I'll make sure to do that."

Frank nodded, turned in a circle next to Alexander's body, and said some words as they both disappeared in a burst of electrical energy.

"He certainly hasn't changed much," Cynder said. "Thank you for not letting him kill Alexander."

"You're welcome," Grey said with a slight nod. "I hope your Wyvern can internalize the lesson. Young dragons have been known to be somewhat dense."

"Again, part of the package," Cynder said. "We're not used to facing existential threats in the form of thorny lizards."

"Few are," Grey said. "Never judge a beating by the cover."

"Dragons rarely, if ever, experience beatings, Warden."

"Still it's a bad policy to put your life on the line based on how an adversary appears," Grey said. "Good and lethal things have a tendency to come in small, volatile packages."

"Agreed," Cynder said. "That being said, we have matters to discuss."

Grey nodded.

"We're going to resolve this Regina-Maledicta issue, but we're going to need your participation," Grey said. "You on board?"

"Do I have a choice?"

"Not really, no," Grey said. "You want this resolved, just like we do. The only difference is the how."

"True, I prefer the scorched earth process," she said. "An enemy dispatched today is one less enemy to face in the future. Regina has declared herself to be my enemy."

"I agree with you in principle, but Regina is in this situation because of your Wyvern over there," Grey said, motioning to Beatrix. "Correct?"

"Yes and no," Cynder said. "When Regina's life hung in the balance, it was Sebastian who opted to save her. My Wyvern did so with the understanding that Sebastian would bear the responsibility for any consequences from that action. Ask him and hear the truth."

"That true?" Grey asked, looking at me. "You gave your word to Beatrix you'd take responsibility for whatever action Regina took?"

"A dragon does not ask for permission," I said, measuring my words. "A dragon acts and deals with the consequences, whatever they may be."

Beatrix nodded with a slight smile.

"That a yes?" Grey asked. "Or you plan on sharing more dragon wisdom?"

"Yes, I told Beatrix to neutralize the gem," I continued. "I gave her my word I would deal with the consequences of that choice."

"*We* did," Tiger added. "Regina was once one of us. Once a Stray Dog, always a Stray Dog, even when they lose their way."

"Regina has turned against the Directive," Cynder asked. "I heard about your run-in earlier on the FDR. She does not feel the same way about either of you."

"Doesn't matter," Tiger said. "She's one of us. We will deal with her."

"Fine," Grey said, looking at Cynder. "You want Regina neutralized and Maledicta destroyed, I have a counter-proposal. One that could work for all of us."

"Which is?"

"Sebastian and Tiger deal with Regina and her neutralization," Grey said. "As for Maledicta, your real issue there is Mura, who's been trying to take it over ever since Calum led them."

"He has been ineffective in that endeavor," Cynder said. "However, he may find success with Regina at the helm of their organization."

"He's just biding his time with Regina, but he'll make a move soon and usurp Maledicta from her grasp and influence. It's just a matter of time."

"What do you propose?" Cynder asked. "You have an alternative?"

"Help the Directive confront and deal with Regina," Grey said, glancing at us. "I'll deal with Mura, which leaves the path open for you."

"Remove the head, and Maledicta will be leaderless," she said. "They will disperse like Umbra before them."

"Something like that," Grey said. "Most of them are rank and file."

"Which makes them aimless."

"Well, if you're feeling forward-thinking," Grey added, "you can install one of your own Wyvern over a leaderless Maledicta. He can provide direction and deal with the contracts you consider beneath your Nine. They handle the grunt work, we avoid wholesale killing, and you increase the size of your organization with your people running it. Win-win all around."

"That could work," Cynder said pensively. "I had been prepared to allow Regina and Maledicta to co-exist with the Nine under my direction until she bypassed the failsafes in the Sacred Amethyst and declared war on me."

"You still can—just without Regina," Grey said. "As for the leader, perhaps you can install a particular Wyvern who needs to have some additional humility instilled into his thick skull?"

"Alexander will consider it a demotion," Beatrix said. "But he will suffer the humiliation after his behavior here today, in order to appease you, Lady Cynder."

Cynder nodded as she mulled it over.

"What if Sebastian can't save Regina?" Cynder asked. "Her restoration is not a foregone conclusion."

"Then I will deal with her," I said. "Whatever steps need to be taken, we will do what needs to be done."

"I'll be there to make sure he does what needs to be done," Grey said. "So will you."

"Me?" Cynder said. "What would you have me do? I have no concern for either party outside of how their actions influence my organization."

"Spoken like a true dragon," Grey said. "I'm not asking you to take an active role."

"We can only be what we are," Cynder said. "I am true to my nature. I refuse to operate under a delusion."

"Nor would I ask you to," Grey said. "A dragon is going to be a dragon. We all default to who we truly are in the end."

"Then?"

"You're going to answer Regina's challenge."

She paused, giving Grey's words some thought.

"I see," she said. "You, Grey, you are a devious man,"

"I prefer to think of it as being unorthodox," he said. "Will you do it?"

"If I answer her challenge, she will be hard-pressed to refuse."

"Impossible, even," Grey said. "She needs to prove she's stronger than you, than Mura. She needs to show them that she can control Maledicta *and* the Shadows of this city."

"She will bring her forces to bear, and you three can execute your plan," Cynder said with a cunning smile. "You're actually using me as bait."

"Is there a problem?" Grey asked.

"None at all, well done," Cynder said with a nod. "Char would be proud. Remind me never to stand against you in warfare. You think just like a dragon."

"I'll take that as a compliment," Grey said. "Good, we're in agreement. Sebastian, when?"

"Tonight," I said. "Like you said, we're on a tight schedule. The sooner we confront Regina, the sooner we can undo the damage of the gem."

"*If* you can undo the damage," Cynder said. "It may be too late. You *must* be prepared for that possibility."

"I am," I said. "I'm prepared for every possibility."

"We shall see," Cynder said. "I will make the arrangements for tonight. Do you have a preference of location for this meet?"

"We need somewhere we can limit the collateral damage to non-combatants and still gather large numbers without being noticed," I said. "It has to be open while providing cover."

"I know just the place," Cynder said, heading to the door

with Beatrix in tow. "I will call you once the time and place is set."

"We'll be ready."

"That remains to be seen."

Cynder and Beatrix exited the Dive.

TWENTY-FIVE

Grey headed behind the bar and brewed more Death Wish, before heading back to the kitchen and having the chef prepare some food for us while we waited for Cynder to contact us.

"How long to midnight?" Tiger asked. "Aren't we cutting it a little close?"

"Time is not on our side here," I said. "We have a few hours still. All the preparation that needed to be done has been done. We need to take action, and we need to do it now, without hesitation."

"Rationally, I understand that," she said as Grey brought out a large tray of delicious-smelling food. "Emotionally, in my gut, I hope we're not making a mistake."

"The only mistake would be inaction."

She nodded.

Grey placed the tray on a table and invited us to eat. It was an assortment of meats and breads. I hadn't realized how hungry I had been, until the appetizing aroma of the food reached my nostrils.

"Eat," Grey said, pointing to the tray and taking a large

portion for himself. "Fuel up. Fighting on an empty stomach is never recommended."

We took his advice to heart and enjoyed the food.

"Your duster," I said, after we had eaten and the chef had removed the tray. "It's special, I just can't pinpoint how. The runes seem ancient, mostly beyond my level of understanding."

Grey looked down at his duster. He had put it on shortly after finishing his meal. The runes shimmered with latent energy.

"They're proto-runes, and the duster itself follows the principle of time and relative dimension in space," Grey said. "Basically, it's larger on the inside."

"Larger on the inside?" Tiger asked. "Doesn't that violate certain laws of magic?"

"I'm sure it violates a few laws," Grey said. "I've learned several things in my years as a Night Warden. You don't argue about the existence of items that save your life, or the people that create them."

"So it *does* act as a portal," I said. "Do you know its outer capacity, or rather, its inner capacity?"

"No," Grey said, shaking his head. "I haven't had a method of exploring its dimensional limits, but I'll ask Aria if there is a way to measure its inner dimensions."

"Aria?" I said. "*She* made your duster, not Heka?"

"Heka is one of the best at weapons," Grey said. "But the runes required for my duster required extensive knowledge of the ancient runes. Heka doesn't have that knowledge…at least not yet."

I nodded, glancing over at his duster.

"Regarding the resilience of your duster, have you tested that aspect of it?" I asked. "I realize that may be more difficult than measuring its inner dimensions, since it would require active stress testing."

"I could help you with that," Tiger said. "I still have to stress test my claws."

"Thanks for the offer, but I'm going to pass," he said, raising a hand. "I haven't tried to measure its indestructibility for obvious reasons. It would mean intentionally placing myself in life-threatening situations. I do enough of that unintentionally, I'm not exactly eager to do it on purpose."

"Understood," I said. "I have to confess, I tried to read your energy signature when we first arrived in the Dive."

"I know."

"You know?"

"I'm a Night Warden, Eyes," he said with a small smile. "I wouldn't be very good at being a Warden or last very long on the streets, if I couldn't tell when someone was trying to read my signature."

"My apologies."

"None needed," he said, waving my words away. "Let me guess, you got a blank? Too much interference to get an accurate energy signature?"

"Yes," I said. "Why is that?"

"Darkspirit, my blade," he said. "The most you're going to sense is energy and power, but it won't be accurate."

"Your blade is that powerful?" Tiger asked. "How?"

"It's not the blade," Grey said. "It's the goddess residing inside the blade that gives it, and me, power. We're bonded and she keeps me alive."

"She keeps you alive?" Tiger asked. "The sword keeps you alive?"

"Yes, that's why the energy signature you read is off by several orders of magnitude. You're not just reading my energy signature, you're reading *our* signature, and you're not even getting her complete signature."

"That makes more sense now," Tiger said. "Can you even read a goddess' complete energy signature?"

"Without frying your brain? Unlikely," Grey said, looking at me. "Now, I have a question for you."

"Of course," I said. "Ask."

"I scanned you when you entered the Dive as well."

"You did?" I said. "I didn't notice you reading my signature."

"I'm a little older than you," he said. "Refer back to my earlier statement about being a Night Warden. I have to be able to read a signature without the target knowing what I'm doing. Many times, my life and the lives of my team depended on my being able to pull that off successfully."

"Understood," I said. "Subterfuge kept you alive."

"Exactly. Now, where did you learn the stasis darkcast?" he asked. "I know you're not a darkmage—none in your Directive have chosen to walk that path—yet here you sit with one of the three shared darkcasts. How?"

"I needed a way to stop Regina long enough to get her to Ivory."

"If it's not too late."

"If we stopped her in time, yes."

"This is not the kind of cast you can just pick up in a local sect," Grey said, after taking a pull from his fresh mug of coffee. I had noticed that he ingested criminal amounts of Death Wish. "Who taught it to you?"

"Dexter Montague," I said, believing that full disclosure worked best with those whom you were going to share a battlefield. "He used something called a transmutational teleport to accelerate the process."

He placed his mug down and gave me a hard stare before speaking again.

"You're insane," he said. "That methodology was discontinued because it either produced vegetables or murderous maniacal mages bent on killing everyone."

"Dexter did make mention of the risks."

"Before or after the procedure?"

"Before."

"And you did it anyway?"

"My first choice is to try and *save* Regina—not go scorched earth, like Cynder, and obliterate her," I said with an edge in my voice. "I still think she has a chance."

Grey raised a hand in surrender and nodded.

"I'm not attacking you," he said, his voice soft as he looked away. "I know what it is to face that choice. I also know what it is to fail to save the person you love. I wasn't ready, I hope you are."

"I'm not," I said, "but it won't stop me from making that choice, should it come to that."

"Do you know how to disable the darkcast?"

"Yes," I said. "Its inner workings are unpleasant, being a shared cast makes it complicated to stop it."

"I'll keep an eye out for you, just in case," he said, taking another sip from his cup. "It's an easy cast to get wrong and then you melt your brain in the process, right before you check out from this life."

Judging from her expression, Tiger seemed uncomfortable with my using a darkcast.

"How dangerous exactly is this darkcast?" Tiger asked, glancing at me. "Real risks, not theoretical."

Grey gave me an evaluating look before speaking.

"If he survived a transmutational teleport, he has a better chance than most. He should be able to cast it and come back from that intact," he said, glancing at me as he explained. "But I'm not going to sugarcoat it; that cast, before it was banned, was used during moments of conflict by all sides. The results"—he looked off into the past for a few seconds and took another swig from his mug—"the results were horrific. No one on either side can justify its use."

Tiger looked at me.

"You sure about this?" she asked. "I know you want to save Regina, but it may be too late."

"We won't know that until we face her," I said. "I don't want to give up on her, unless there is no other option."

"You're not going to change his mind on this," Grey said, shaking his head. "My fellow Night Wardens tried to talk me down from releasing an entropic dissolution in a populated city more than once. They failed. I did it anyway and nearly died in the process."

"An entropic dissolution in a city is insane," Tiger said. "You cast that even when you knew the danger?"

"I did," he said. "All that mattered was saving Jade. I failed, and truly, if I'm being honest, I did die that day. It just hasn't caught up to me—yet. He's on this path and he's going to walk it, with or without us. I'd rather be there than let him face this alone. I know you feel the same."

"I do," she said as my phone rang. "We see this through to the end."

I picked up my phone, connected the call, and put it on speaker.

"Where and when?"

"Tonight, as you requested," Cynder said. "Sheep Meadow, in the Park. Do you know where it is?"

"I do," I said. "Not much cover there. You'll be exposed in the center of an open space."

"I believe that's the plan," she said. "I got the distinct impression Regina doesn't trust me...Imagine that."

"How many of your people are you bringing?" I asked. "I'm fairly certain she will be bringing all of Maledicta."

"None," she said, her voice firm. "Let me reiterate my role here to avoid any confusion. I am the bait and will act as such. If I had any intention on confronting Regina directly, I would have done so by now, and we would not be having this conversation. You'd be making burial arrangements of whatever was left of her."

"You will be walking into an ambush," I explained. "The Meadow will be filled with Maledicta."

"Little brother, I am a *dragon,*" she said. "I formed and lead the Nine. I don't need an army. I *am* an army. I will bring her to the designated place, and you will take it from there. I will await in my Eyrie to hear the outcome of your confrontation."

"So you won't help us?" Tiger said, an accusing tone in her voice. "Us three against all of Maledicta?"

"No, I won't help you beyond what I have just stated, and yes, it's you three against all of Maledicta," she said. "You accepted the mark, you are charkin. You also have Grey, the last Night Warden standing with you. As you have witnessed earlier, I have no need to assure you of his power or his willingness to wield it. For all intents and purposes, tonight, you are dragons. You stand or fall on your merits and abilities, as a dragon should."

It wasn't lost on me that she chose Sheep Meadow. That location in Central Park was also close to Ivory's Tower, which, if we managed to capture Regina, meant we would be close to the help we needed to remove the gem. Cynder didn't mention it, but I made a mental note to address that privately with her.

"Thank you," I said. "I do appreciate your participation and assistance in this."

"I strongly advise against using your vehicles," Cynder said. "Grey's vehicle is currently under surveillance by the Councils. It seems you have angered some powerful individuals, Warden."

Grey shrugged.

"I'm popular that way," he said. "What about the Directive's Tank?"

"That vehicle is being sought by most of the NYTF for their stunt driving on the FDR today," she said. "Find alternative means of travel."

"We will," I said. "We have a few preparations to make in the meantime. See you at midnight."

"Do not be late," she said. "It could be fatal."

"For you?" Tiger asked. "I thought you were an *army*?"

"Pettiness does not become a charkin," Cynder said. "The danger is not present for me."

"Then who?" Tiger asked. "We're already stepping into a blender on this meet."

"For Regina, child," Cynder said. "If she tries to launch an attack on me, I will respond in kind. I will not be merciful. There can only be one outcome from our conflict. She will *not* be walking away. Do not be late."

Cynder ended the call.

TWENTY-SIX

"Isn't she just pleasant?" Tiger said. "Sheep Meadow will be a killing field. We'll be exposed without cover. Why would she pick that location?"

"Few reasons," Grey said. "It gives Regina and Maledicta a sense of superiority. They'll feel like Cynder made a strategic mistake and that they have the advantage, because there is nowhere for Cynder to hide, even at night. She's a sitting duck, or dragon, in this case."

"I can't believe they think superior numbers will work against Cynder," I said. "They are underestimating her power."

"I doubt they've ever faced a mature dragon like Cynder," Grey said. "You noticed earlier she didn't bleed when I activated the defenses to level two, but the Wyvern did?"

"I noticed," I said. "She was feeling the effects of the defenses, but even when you increased them to level three, she was dealing with them with little discomfort."

"If I were serious about stopping her, I'd have to crank them up to level four, and cast," Grey said. "She's no slouch."

"Not level five?" Tiger asked. "What is that level for? What kind of enemies do you have?"

"Level five," Grey said, his voice softer, but no less dangerous. "I designed that level for divine guests that feel nothing can stop them."

"Divine guests?"

"Gods, yes," he said. "Level five in the Dive, plus my sword and a few specific darkcasts can adjust that attitude of invulnerability in a hurry."

"Wouldn't that impact you as well?" I asked. "Level five sounds lethal, even for you."

"If I ever activate level five, I'm not expecting to walk out of the Dive," he said. "Then again, neither is anyone else. That level is doomsday."

"Understood," I said. "I'm glad you didn't need to use it today."

"Me too," he said, looking at me. "Now, how do we play this? I noticed that Sheep Meadow, while being a potential killing field like Tiger astutely pointed out, is close to Ivory. Was that your doing?"

"No," I said. "However, I did notice the proximity too."

"Right then, that's Cynder's way of helping," he said. "No one else is even going to attempt to remove that gem Regina merged with in this city, unless it's someone like Ivory. It's too risky and the potential fallout for tampering with an artifact of that caliber is liable to get whoever tries, dead in short order."

I nodded.

"Ivory is on 58th between Broadway and 7th Avenue," I said, thinking out loud. "Sheep Meadow sits between 65th and 69th just off Central Park West. Close enough to place Ivory close by in the Park and ready to move once we immobilize Regina."

"Can she do it?" Grey asked. "I know she's old and not

exactly human—does she have the ability to deal with the gem?"

"I believe so," I said, without going into too much detail about what exactly Ivory was. "She is ancient and has demonstrated the capacity to handle something of this magnitude."

He took another pull from his mug.

"Grey, I mean no offense, but why do you drink so much Death Wish?" I asked. "You do realize those amounts can't be healthy?"

"There's no such thing as too much Death Wish," he said, with a grin. "Especially not the way I make it."

"I stand corrected," I said. "As I said, no offense intended."

His expression became serious before continuing.

"None taken," he said, looking down at the inky liquid in his mug. "I have to cast tonight, I may even need to let my sword take over for a short time."

"Is that wise?" I asked. "Doesn't that place you and more importantly the city in danger?"

"Only if I lose control," he answered. "I have contingencies in place if that ever happens. Frank may be on leave, but he is always vigilant when I'm on a mission. There are others too, who know that if I ever lose it, they have instructions to stop me, by any means necessary."

"You live under a sword of Damocles," I said, getting a glimpse of what made him act the way he did. "And the coffee?"

"The coffee allows me to keep my wits about me when the ice pick of pain that gets shoved into the base of my brain every time I cast explodes," he said. "It allows me to retain control and resist."

"Resist?" Tiger asked. "Resist what?"

"Her," he said. "I can resist the invitations from the bloodthirsty goddess in my sword." He glanced at me. "You have no idea how accurate you were in your description of a sword of Damocles."

"Why?" Tiger asked. "Why do you live this way?"

"Because I'm not doing it for me," Grey said. "I have people who count on me being here, I have people on the streets whose voices remain unheard. I still have a city to protect and a Night Warden to train and prepare. I do this because I am a Night Warden and I took a vow. I do it because I honor my word."

"I can respect that," Tiger said. "We feel the same way in the Directive."

"Good, we're on the same page then," he said, standing up. "I hope I don't have to bury any of you tonight."

"I share the same sentiment," I said. "Do you have a method for us to get to Sheep Meadow, or should I procure alternative transportation?"

"Too risky," he said. "We convene on the second floor at thirty minutes before midnight, and I'll get us there. I suggest you stay in the Dive. If the NYTF is looking for your Tank, it means they're looking for you, too. The last thing you want right now is to get hung up with Ramirez about how destruction runs in your family."

"Or worse, explaining it all to Ursula," Tiger said. "That is not a conversation I'm looking forward to having."

"I strongly advise you *do* call her and explain," Grey said. "That's one bear you don't want upset at you. Well, *more* upset at you."

"Good point," I said. "Does your home have a training area and a casting circle?"

"Second floor," Grey said, standing up. "Feel free to use the facilities. Avoid the third floor, those are my living quarters and the defenses on that level will blast you to dust if you try to go up there without authorization."

"Got it, avoid the third floor," I said. "Any other areas off-limits?"

"Front door is sealed inside and out," he said. "The neutral zone is currently closed for the night. Anyone who needs to know, knows. We won't be getting any unwanted guests. Other than those two locations, you have access to the rest of the place."

"Thank you," I said. "What will you be doing in the meantime?"

"Unlike you, I can wander outside these walls," he said with slight grin, then became serious again. "I'm going to mentally prepare to cast, I need to make sure my people know what's going down tonight, and see if I can get some reinforcements. Three against all of Maledicta are not 'walking away' kind of odds."

"Reinforcements?" Tiger said. "Can you scramble a small army?"

"Why?" Grey said, heading to the stairs and climbing. "Didn't you hear Cynder? You two are dragons. You're all the army we need."

"That's not even remotely funny," Tiger said. "I'm not looking forward to facing all of Maledicta with just you two."

"I'll work on it," Grey said, pausing on the stairs and turning to face us. "Oh, one more thing, Eyes—you being who you are, I feel the need to advise you not to blow up any part of my house."

"I'll make sure to avoid demolition of the premises."

"Good," he said. "I've dealt with enough unwanted renovations in the past. How about we set a new precedent of no property damage?"

"I'll work on it."

"You do that."

He disappeared from sight with a short laugh as he climbed the stairs.

TWENTY-SEVEN

"He's not just an old mage," Tiger said when he was out of sight. "He's a cranky, smartass, old mage."

"Who has earned the right to be a cranky, smartass, old mage," I said. "I wasn't exactly pleased when Regina blew a hole in the Church. No one likes to have their home obliterated."

"Speaking of Regina, you're going to try the darkcast again, aren't you?" she asked. "That's why you asked for a circle?"

"I need to make sure I *can* cast with ease when needed," I said. "It felt difficult on the FDR. It will be a catastrophic failure if I wait until we confront her to see if I can cast it, and then realize I can't."

"How are you going to manage to cast it without a target?" she asked. "Isn't it a shared cast?"

"Yes," I said. "There's...a workaround."

"Why does this workaround sound more dangerous than the original cast?" she said. "What is this *workaround?*"

"I can do this if I'm inside a training circle," I said. "It has the potential to be chancy, but I think it's possible. It's certainly safer than trying it outside of a circle, or in the heat of battle."

"You still haven't explained what this *workaround* is," she said. "Break it down for me using simple words."

"I have to step into my mind palace."

She stared at me with an incredulous look.

"A mind palace?" she said. "An actual mental construct?"

"Think of it more as a mental simulation," I said. "When I was starting my mage studies, every mage was obligated to create one to run the casts we had learned, without actually casting them."

"But?" she said. "I know you, Seb, there is a *but* in there somewhere. You took this mind palace construct and changed it, didn't you?"

"Somewhat," I admitted. "The original construct was inadequate."

"Of course, it was," she said, exasperated. "Why would you settle for normal, when you can create strange? What did you do?"

"I merely adjusted the parameters to allow for time compression," I said. "Well, I didn't exactly come up with the idea, but I did improve on the general concept."

"Who came up with this bright idea?" she asked. "Let me guess, Dexter?"

"No, Dexter gave me some much needed insight," he said. "But he didn't conceive it. The original idea of simulating time compression on a mage brain in order to practice casts was first postulated by Professor Ziller in a theoretical paper. I merely took his ideas, approached them from a different perspective and made them work."

"What different perspective?"

"Have you ever noticed that when you feel close to death

or face a life-threatening event, time seems to slow down?" I asked. "Yet, at the same time, your entire life seems to flash before your eyes in a moment?"

"If I say no, will you drop this dangerous-sounding idea?" she asked. "Because the longer you keep explaining, the more I think this is a bad idea."

"It's perfectly safe—as long as I stay in the circle," I said. "You do understand the concept though, yes?"

"I get the whole life flashing before your eyes thing, yes."

"The process I discovered lets you direct that flow of information," I said. "You can control what specific content flows before your eyes."

"What is the danger?"

"It's minimal."

"That's not a description of the danger," she said, her voice a warning. "What is the risk?"

"Irreparable acceleration followed by acute deceleration of mental acuity," I said. "The world will appear to speed up and then go extraordinarily slow...permanently."

"I'm beginning to think you're already permanently stuck in the extraordinarily slow phase of this process," she said. "Are you insane?"

"I survived the transmutational teleportation," I said. "This is much safer than that."

She punched me in the stomach...hard. The blow forced me to take a few steps back. The fact that I wasn't coughing up blood or any of my internal organs meant she had pulled the strike.

"Did you feel that?"

"Of course I felt that," I said with a short gasp. "What was that for?"

"Just making sure you still feel pain," she said. "You nearly died during that transmutational teleport and more importantly, Dexter was the one casting it on you. I trust his skill with dicey casts—you know, due to the whole age and experience thing. You, not so much."

"I am amazed by your faith in my skills," I said, feigning offense. "I have cast this many times in the past. Contrary to what you think, I do know what I'm doing."

"I know you do," she said, softening her tone. "I don't want you, in your effort to save Regina, to risk everything to the point of damaging yourself...or death."

"This is why you're going to help me."

"I'm going to do what now?"

"I'm going to simulate the shared darkcast without the energy component," I said. "Together, while we are in the circle, I will run the darkcast and disable it multiple times under time compression."

"So now you want to share the danger with me?" she said, shaking her head. "Pass, thanks, but no. I like my perception of time to remain nice and stable. Not sped up and slowed down."

"You won't be exposed to any danger," I said. "You are there as my failsafe."

"Can I be your failsafe with a fist?"

"Only if I'm not responsive to other forms of deterrence," I answered. "I'd prefer a less violent failsafe, if at all possible."

"If you're going to take these risks, I don't know if I can do less violent," she said. "Take it, or no simulation."

"Thank you for your assistance then," I said. "Let's go see what kind of circle Grey has available for us to use."

"How long is this going take?" she asked. "We do have a timetable to be aware of."

"By the time we're done, we will still have plenty of time to get ready and join Grey to travel to Sheep Meadow."

"That works. Before we do this, you set up Ivory, and I'll

call Ursula and the rest of the Directive to let them know what's going on," she said. "Let's get that done, and then we can see if this darkcast simulation will really work."

"Agreed," I said. "I'll come find you when I'm done setting up Ivory for tonight."

TWENTY-EIGHT

I dialed the number for Ivory's direct line.

She answered after several rings.

"Do you have her, and why are you calling me when you should be here if you do?"

"We are meeting tonight at midnight," I said. "How are we on time?"

"Cutting it close," she said. "Where are you meeting? Is she willing to surrender?"

"Sheep Meadow, and it's unlikely she will surrender willingly."

"I see," Ivory said. "You want me close by, yes?"

"If it's not too much trouble?" I asked. "Sheep Meadow is not far from your Tower."

"If I do this for you, I want something from you in return."

It was always dangerous to make deals with ifrit. They were exceptional at creating and finding loopholes in every one of their transactions.

"Yes or no?" she asked, sensing my hesitation. "Will you honor my request?"

"Yes," I said after a few more moments. "Only me, no requests from anyone else in the Directive. If you can agree to these terms, then, yes."

"Good," she said. "If I do this, no matter the outcome to your love—success or failure—you will make me part of the Treadwell Supernatural Directive."

I was stunned silent for a few seconds.

"You're an ifrit," I said. "Why would you want to join the Directive?"

"My reasons are my own," she said. "Yes or no?"

"A decision like that cannot be imposed on the others," I said. "There is a selection process. The rest of the Directive must agree by unanimous vote."

"Which will be heavily influenced by your recommendation, yes?"

"Yes," I admitted. "My endorsement will very likely sway the rest of the Directive."

"Good, do you agree?" she asked again. "Success or failure, you will present me as a candidate to join the Directive?"

I was still mildly shocked at the request, but I didn't see the harm in making the suggestion.

"On one more condition," I said. "If you can answer this for me, I will put my full weight behind endorsing your candidacy into the Directive."

"Yes?"

"Success or failure, you tell me your reason for wanting to be in the Directive," I said. "Yes or no?"

It was her turn to hesitate.

"Yes," she said after an extended pause. "But only to you. No one else must know the reason."

"Agreed," I said, still slightly perplexed. "Do you know where Tavern on the Green is located?"

"Yes," she said. "I am familiar with this place. Do you require I set up a makeshift infirmary at this location?"

"If possible, yes," I said. "I also need you to mask your presence along with the presence of your security. Is that possible?"

"No one will know we are there," she said. "I will bring two of my security, as is my custom."

A thought struck me in that moment.

"Ivory? Can you mobilize more than two of your security?"

"Of course, but I rarely need more than two," she said. "If I am being honest, one is usually enough for any of my ventures out of my facility. Why do you ask?"

I explained the reason for my request.

"That can be done," she said, becoming somber. "But I cannot guarantee they will comply. Do you take responsibility for any loss of life?"

"I do."

"Very well," she said with a nod. "I can submit your request. If they agree, it will take them some time to assemble. They will require ten minutes."

"Ten minutes, I understand. Thank you," I said. "I will see you soon."

"No thanks are required," she answered. "Move with haste to save your woman."

I ended the call with the certainty that we had just tipped the scales slightly in our favor.

I only hoped it was enough.

Several minutes later, Tiger joined me on the second floor.

"Ursula is less than happy," Tiger said, "but she was glad I called."

"Did she deduce we were involved in the FDR situation?"

"One word," Tiger said. "Cameras. DAMNED has them all over the city. Says it was next to impossible to make out the murdered out Tank, but she wanted us to know that she knows it was us."

"Is she going to pursue this?"

"No," Tiger said, shaking her head. "Said to help Regina and get Maledicta off the streets, and she will develop sudden onset selective amnesia."

"We can do that," I said. "And the Directive?"

"Activated the Rogue Wolf Protocol," she said. "They will lock down the Church, and those that can assist will be on site in the Park."

"Good," I said. "I may have gotten us some help to make this evening go smoother, but it's going to take time."

"How much time?"

"We only need to hold out for ten minutes," I said. "If she comes through."

"*If* she comes through? You're not certain?"

"Nothing in life is certain," I said. "I made a request. She may or may not honor it."

"That is a long time in a battle," she said. "Who is insane enough to help us?"

I explained the request I made of Ivory and what she wanted in return. Tiger thought about it for a few moments and nodded.

"I don't see a problem with her being a Stray Dog," Tiger said. "With the number of times she's patched us up, you especially, she's practically one of us by now anyway."

"My reasoning exactly," I replied, heading to the stairs. "You ready to try this?"

"Lead the way," she said, following me upstairs. "I'm warning you now—I see things go sideways, I'm making sure the simulation is over. We clear?"

"Understood," I said as we reached Grey's training area. It held an ample amount of conventional training equipment as well as two large casting circles. One was specifically designed for teleports, and the other, from what I could decipher of the runes around its edge, was created for general casts. I pointed to the second circle. "This one."

"Where do you want me?" she asked. "Do I go in the circle with you?"

"Yes," I said. "I will cast the simulation, you will be tethered to me. Inside but not part of it. That way you can monitor my state of mind and remove me from the simulation if needed."

"I certainly will if needed," she said with a devious smile. "With the utmost prejudice."

"No need to look so enthusiastic about pummeling me," I said. "A gentle nudge should suffice."

"I'm not the gentle nudge type," she said, cracking her knuckles. "Be careful in there."

"I will be."

I sat in the center of the circle and Tiger sat inside, facing me but near the edge. The circle, along with the second floor training area was fairly large. This particular circle was filled with runes, most of which I could decipher.

As I sat in the circle, I saw the outer edge of the circle become a deep violet. Tiger raised an eyebrow, but remained motionless where she was.

I focused my breath and mind as I closed my eyes.

Within moments, the second floor of Grey's training area slowly vanished, leaving me sitting in a large marble palace resembling a small Taj Mahal.

Once the mind palace was complete, I opened my eyes and took in the wonder of architecture I had created in my mind. It wasn't an exact replica, since I had added my own embellishments and adaptations.

It was close enough to be amazing.

The white marble glistened in the low sunlight of my imagination as I recalled that I had created this mind palace from the most memorable palace that had come to my mind at the time.

I slowly stood, taking in the magnificence of the ancient mausoleum that now served as my mind palace.

I stepped into a large courtyard and felt Tiger's presence just outside the palace, an ever-present presence of strength and power. An actual Bengal tiger padded across the courtyard and let out a low growl in my direction.

It was enormous and completely focused on me.

"Well, that not's on the nose at all," I muttered to myself. "She'd love to see herself depicted as an actual tiger in my imagination."

I gave the tiger a short nod. It let out a low rumble and remained focused on me as I sat on a large mat designed for meditation.

With a quick exhalation, I got my breath under control and began the first series of gestures required for the stasis darkcast. I flowed through it fairly smoothly, giving myself credit for executing a difficult cast under the watchful claws of an enormous tiger.

I repeated the gestures, each time adding to the sequence until I had completed the entire cast. That was the easy part. Now came the complicated section.

I spread my arms and slowly brought my hands close together. In-between my hands, I formed a crystal clock. Once the clock was fully formed, I removed my hands and let it float off to one side.

The tiger kept track of every move I made as it laid down.

The analog clock hovered in the air just to the right of my field of view. I placed a finger on the minute hand and held my breath. Realizing the futility of such an action in this place made me chuckle and shake my head self-consciously for a few seconds.

I brought my finger down, causing the minute hand to

race around the crystal clock face. Looking off into the horizon, I took a moment to observe and marvel at the rapidly rising and falling sun.

I began the cast again as I accessed the details of the stasis darkcast stored in my memory. The information in my mind surrounded me in an exploded view, the symbols and runes hanging in the air all around me as I stood there, deconstructing the darkcast.

After a few seconds, the rising and falling sun became part of the background, forgotten and ignored for the symbols floating around me.

I stepped in and around the symbols around me, moving them to one side and rearranging the order as my thought process accelerated.

Through it all, the tiger stared at me. Soon, it too faded into the background.

After countless days, my hands and mind were moving in a blur. I could form the cast, stop it, and execute it forwards and backwards. I could start it from any point in the cast and continue forward or move backward as I desired.

What was, at first, a tentative exploratory tracing of symbols, became over countless days, months, and years, an expert mastery of the darkcast.

I was done.

I had attained a firm grasp of the darkcast and could now cast it whenever I needed it. With a slow exhalation, I reached for the crystal clock. Its circular body hummed and vibrated as the hand raced around its face.

I placed it between my hands and focused, willing the acceleration of time around me to slow. The clock nearly vibrated itself out of my hands in protest as I held it tight.

That can't be good.

Nothing happened.

The hands didn't slow at all and I became concerned.

The tiger, which up until this moment looked vaguely disinterested and frankly appeared bored, suddenly became very alert and stood.

Again, I tried to slow the flow of time on the clock face, cognizant that it wasn't real, but only a construct I had created to help me grasp the concept of time in my mind palace.

It flew out of my hands and sailed off into the distance.

Bloody hell, that's really not good.

I saw parts of my mind palace began to shudder and fall apart, revealing the blackness of space and the brilliance of stars in the gaps. I saw stars and galaxies whirl in the distance and realized there was a good chance I was losing my mind.

More sections of my mind palace fell apart, and I glanced at the tiger which was running now, trying to reach me, but the courtyard had elongated, increasing the distance between us.

Time was dilating while simultaneously compressing. I realized that I could only take so much more of this, before I suffered a fracturing of my mind.

I sat down and closed my eyes, focusing my mind. I ignored the shattering sounds of cracking marble and only focused on the singular point of my breath.

As I managed to get it briefly under control, I made the mistake of opening my eyes in my haste to leave this place. All around me, the marble exhibited huge cracks and gaps in the stone.

I nearly lost control again when I turned to look at an enormous crack racing along the floor, headed my way. Out of the corner of my eye, a flash of orange and black crossed my vision. I felt the impact of a large tiger claw across my face as Grey's training area reformed under my feet.

I was back.

TWENTY-NINE

"Slash me sideways!" Tiger yelled. "What the hell was that? You said it as safe!"

"It was, it is," I said, rubbing my face. "I don't know what happened. At no point did I introduce any stasis energy into the darkcast."

"Then what happened?" she demanded. "One moment you were doing your best yoga instructor imitation, the next, it appeared you were slipping away."

"I was," I said, still rubbing my face. "Out of curiosity, what did you hit me with?"

"My fist," she said. "I warned you I would if I saw something going wrong."

"You did," I said, getting to my feet as I searched my memory. "If it's any consolation, I learned the stasis darkcast."

"It's not," she said. "You need to stop taking these risks, Seb. What would've happened if I wasn't here?"

"Nothing good, I think," I said, deflecting to avoid telling her I would have lost my mind and ended up stark raving mad. "I would have most likely been stuck in my mind palace."

"You...are a horrible liar," she said as Grey walked into the training area. She turned to face him. "Are we ready to go?"

"What's the yelling about?" Grey asked. "If you have something you need to air out, do it now." He looked at his watch. "It's a quarter past eleven. We don't have time to drag baggage into battle."

"No baggage," Tiger said, her words icy as she stared at me. "Just some people have a tendency to forget that they are not alone out here. That some of us have people who care for them and don't want to see them turn themselves into vegetables."

"Vegetables?" Grey said, looking at me. "We won't have time for a heart to heart once we arrive. Anything you want to say?"

"Nothing," I said, my voice just as icy. "There are some of us who realize that the responsibility they carry forces them to make choices some won't agree with. Those choices do not diminish how much they care."

"I am not going to deliver messages for either of you," Grey said. "Squash this, let's go save Regina and stop Maledicta unless you two would prefer to stay here and bicker so Cynder can go all scorched earth on everyone, dust Regina, all of Maledicta, and be home in time for a warm cup of tea, or whatever it is dragons drink at night."

"I'm sorry," I said. "It was wrong of me to take that risk. It was unnecessary and unwise."

"Damn straight it was," Tiger said. "Sorry for ripping your head off, you deserved it, but I understand why you did what you did."

Grey nodded.

"See, much better now?" he said. "Well, if this whole

Warden gig falls through, maybe I can get a job at the UN and be a diplomat. You two ready?"

We both nodded as he motioned for us to enter the teleportation circle.

"This will feel...a little weird," he said as he gestured. "Keep your hands and feet inside the circle at all times."

Black symbols filled the circle beneath us as it slowly began to rotate. In moments, the floor under us disappeared, and we dropped into a portal of darkness.

We emerged at the edge of Sheep Meadow.

I set the timer on my watch.

In the distance, I could see Cynder walking toward a figure, and my heart skipped a few beats as my breath caught in my throat.

Regina.

The night was deathly silent, but I could sense the multitude of energy signatures around us. Standing next to and just behind Regina, towered an enormous figure which I knew was Mura.

Both were dressed in the signature, light-absorbing Maledicta combat gear—the only difference being the red sleeve of Regina's gear.

"We better get over there before Regina does something terminal she won't have time to regret," Tiger said under her breath as we moved fast. "By the way, we are currently surrounded by Maledicta."

"Not the focus right now," Grey said, pointing forward as we closed the distance. "Stopping that interaction from becoming fatal is. Tiger, can you throw a distraction their way?"

"I can," she said, forming an orb and unleashing it at the biggest target in the center of the Meadow—Mura. "Maybe that will soften him up for you."

Mura twisted his body avoiding the orb and glared at Tiger, who smiled and waved back.

"Unlikely but it's appreciated," Grey said, looking off to the right as he approached Mura at a flank. "Ivory close by?"

"Tavern," I said. "Try not to get dead."

"Same to you," he said and vanished from sight, reappearing nearly ten feet away from Mura. "I'm your huckleberry for this fight, big guy." He motioned to Mura, beckoning the giant to come closer. "Over here."

Mura glanced at Cynder, and I saw the rapid calculations he made. Fighting a dragon was a losing proposition—even for him. Regina would either attack Cynder and win, or more likely would be killed in a failed attempt.

Either scenario benefitted him.

In the meantime, he could crush this mage relic who was taunting him, while Cynder handed him Maledicta. It was flawed logic, but judging from the outward appearance of things, it was the right call.

He was mistaken and would soon find out how some errors could turn deadly in an instant. In this instance, I doubted Mura would leave the Park tonight—alive.

I looked at my watch.

It was midnight exactly.

"Right on time," Cynder called out without turning around. "One minute more and things would have gotten interesting. However, I do commend your punctuality." She looked at a seething Regina and gave her a smile. "Your lover just saved your life, child. My part here is done. Time for me to do something more productive with my time. Sebastian, do fill me in when you can."

"Don't you dare," Regina said. "Face me, Cynder."

Cynder gave her a small headshake.

"This is tired and boring," Cynder said with a short laugh.

"To think you could stand against me—daring, but misguided."

Regina glanced at Tiger and me.

"And if I kill your *charkin*?" she asked. "What will you do then?"

Cynder turned then.

"If you manage to kill even *one* of them, I will face you in combat," Cynder said, glancing at me and giving me a wink. "I find it doubtful, even with your newly acquired gem power, but one can dream. Until then, you're wasting my time. Goodbye."

She turned, took three steps and vanished.

Regina focused on me.

"You have no idea what you've done," she said, enraged. "You cost me everything."

"It was never yours to begin with," I said, raising my hands. "You're not thinking straight. We're here to help you. Let us help you."

"Liar," she said, shaking her head. "You always were jealous of me, of my power and abilities."

"That's not true," I said. "I only had admiration for your abilities and power. This is not you, Regina. Stop this."

"Stop this?" she said, forming a cluster of blades around her. "I'm just getting started." She looked off into the darkness and raised her voice. "Maledicta, my Shadows. Kill the old mage and the woman, but leave this one to me."

"Well, shit," Tiger said, backing up to cover my flank. "This went south in a hurry."

I saw some of the shadows in the trees begin to shift and move. A large group of them were headed toward Grey, while another group headed our way.

"We only need to hold out for ten minutes, apprehend her and then head over to Tavern on the Green," I said under my breath as Tiger stood behind me back to back. "Only ten minutes."

"Ten minutes is a lifetime, Seb," Tiger said. "Do you really think they will show?"

"I don't know," I said as Regina formed more blades around her. "In the meantime, we stay alive."

THIRTY

I formed my karambits, moving forward to intercept Regina.

Tiger unleashed a kinetic wall, violently shoving back any Maledicta closing on our location. I glanced to my right and could hear Grey and Mura exchanging blows.

Mura was wielding a large, rune-covered scimitar that glowed a dull blue. Grey held a blade of darkness and was smiling as he parried Mura's attacks.

His expression concerned me, but I couldn't spare more than half a second on him. Regina closed on me with a snarl as several blades flew by my face.

At first, I thought she had deliberately missed me, then I realized...Regina didn't miss unless she wanted to miss. She wasn't aiming for me.

She was aiming for Tiger.

"Behind you!" I yelled into the night as Tiger threw up another shield. I heard her deflecting the blades away from her back. "Regina, the gem is corrupting you."

"Corrupting me?" she scoffed as she tried to stab my chest. "For the first time in my life, I feel free."

She formed a barrage of blades and surrounded me,

cutting me off from Tiger, who fought the Shadows of Maledicta close to fifty feet away.

"This is not freedom," I said, parrying her attack as I dodged a slash, before moving to the side to deflect two blades from burying themselves in my neck. "You're a slave to that gem. It's killing you."

"Do not lie to me."

"Why would I lie to you?"

"Why would you lie," she said, her voice low and slowly increasing the volume. "Why would you lie! You *would* lie! You lied to me! After everything I did for you, for your precious Directive. Everything I sacrificed, everything I left... for you! I formed the first group, I found the ideal location. It was my casts that created the first sealing runes that protected us. Your Directive wouldn't exist without me, I laid the foundation."

"Yes, you did," I said, keeping my karambits up as I remained in a defensive stance. "That was all you."

"I fought our first threats," she said, her voice far away as she remembered. "How many times did I save members of our Directive?"

"Too many to count," I said, circling. "You saved everyone at least once, myself included."

"Damn right," she said. "Too many to count. I saved the Directive. I helped establish us as a force to be reckoned with in the city, when no one knew who we were. I approached the Councils, I established the accords. I sacrificed everything for the Directive... For you."

"You did," I said, keeping my voice calm and trying to pacify her. "You sacrificed."

"Now...now it's your turn to sacrifice," she said, lowering her voice and remaining still. "Don't worry, my love. I told you, I'm going to set you free from everything that's keeping us apart."

"Regina, don't do this," I said, raising my arms. "You can walk away."

"Walk away?" she mocked. "I'll walk away after I set things right. After I destroy the Directive, starting with Tiger, your second-in-command."

Regina lunged forward and slashed low. I knew it for the feint it was and parried high as a blade dove at my face. Knocking the blade away distracted me long enough for her to get close and drive a fist in my ribs.

She had become stronger.

Much stronger.

The blow knocked me to the side, causing me to lose sight of her for a few seconds. A few seconds was a lifetime when facing a blademaster, worse, when facing a blademaster —corrupted and amplified by a gem deteriorating her mind.

I dodged sideways, avoiding several blades which buried themselves in the ground where I stood seconds earlier. I managed to get unsteadily back to my feet and...right into a punishing kick that launched me several feet away and landed me on my back.

I saw a blur cross my vision as Tiger engaged Regina.

Gathering my wits about me, I arose and raced back into the fray, only to see Regina form several crackling, dark red orbs around her. She unleashed the lethal barrage of orbs at Tiger, who threw up a shield and deflected them to the side.

Using the orbs as a diversion, Regina moving faster than she had ever moved, closed the distance on Tiger and jumped up. As she landed, she buried a fist in Tiger's chest, giving her no time to erect a new shield.

Regina managed to knock Tiger across the grass of the Meadow. She sent several blades after her for good measure. I was about to assist Tiger when Regina hurled another set of blades at me, cutting off my path.

I parried two and ducked under the third which sailed past me.

"Going somewhere, love?" she asked as she approached. "I hope you said your goodbyes to your precious Directive. Tiger won't be seeing another sunrise. In fact, haven't you heard? The Treadwell Supernatural Directive is headed for early retirement. Once I'm done here, I think it's time for church."

I glanced over quickly at where Tiger had fallen fell and saw a lattice of black energy deflect the incoming blades.

Grey had run interference.

"Stop this madness," I said as Regina closed on my position. I could see Maledicta close in on us too. After Tiger's first offensive shield, they had waited in the trees and were stepping into the darkness all around us. This situation was going to become a bloodbath in short order if we didn't shut her and Mura down. "You are going to kill your Shadows."

"They are prepared to die for, Maledicta, for me," she said. "Even now, at the end, you still don't understand."

She took several quick steps forward, slashing with each step. I backpedaled, blocking and deflecting her attacks.

"Why not take the killing blow, Sebastian?" she taunted. "It's the only way this is going to end."

She formed a red orb and launched it at me.

I slashed the air with my karambits and whispered a word of power. The orb exploded on contact, as I sliced through it. In that moment, a roar filled the night as Mura charged at me. Regina dodged back with a laugh as I turned just in time to get hit by the bus that was the giant.

He pounded an elbow into my side, driving the air from my lungs as I slid away. He made to strike down with his blade, when a dark cloud of energy exploded from Grey.

"You made a fatal error," I heard Grey say in a strange voice. One moment he was several feet away, the next he intercepted Mura and nearly buried Darkspirit in his abdomen.

Mura had managed to parry the attack at the last moment, only to realize his error. Grey had formed black orbs and unleashed them. They formed a cordon of black energy around him and shot off into the night.

All around us, Maledicta fell where they stood as the orbs shot through them at phenomenal speed. A few seconds later, only Mura and Regina remained standing on the Meadow. The rest of Maledicta, the ones who remained in the shadows and trees were frozen in place, tendrils of black energy wrapped around their bodies and it appeared they were slowly being siphoned.

Mura charged at Grey.

It was the last mistake he made.

It became abundantly clear he was no longer facing Grey.

Tiger raced to my side and ran past me as she dove at Regina, claws drawn. Regina formed blades in each hand and stopped Tiger in her attack with a smile.

"I'm stronger than you, than all of you," Regina said. "You can't stop me. You're all weak. I will make you realize that truth before the end."

Regina rotated the blades in her hands and backhanded Tiger across the Meadow. Tiger landed hard, rolling for several feet before coming to a sudden stop by a tree.

She didn't move.

Regina was growing stronger and more irrational by the moment.

"Don't worry," Regina said, her voice contemptuous. "She's not dead...not yet."

Regina dematerialized her blades and began walking toward me.

"Look around you, Sebastian," she said, extending an arm. "The Directive is a failed experiment. You're here alone.

Tiger has fallen, the Night Warden can't last much longer without whatever is in him taking over."

"He's stronger than you imagine," I said.

"At this rate, Mura will cut through him with his blade," she continued. "The Warden is strong, but whatever is in him is stronger. He'll lose control soon. It's only a matter of time. Admit the truth and come with me. Relinquish the Directive."

"They don't deserve your hate," I said. "You said it yourself, you helped create the Directive. Why would you do this?"

"Because I can," she hissed. "I created them and I will destroy them. You're right they don't deserve my hate, they all deserve to die. Say goodbye to Tiger."

Regina slashed an arm down.

A group of five blades materialized next to her and raced at the unconscious Tiger.

"No!" I yelled. "Stop!"

"I will, if you relinquish the Directive and join me," she said, turning her head slowly and following the blades with her gaze as they sliced through the night, silent emissaries of death headed for my unconscious second-in-command. "Tick tock, love. Your precious Tiger is running out of time. What will it be, Director? Me or the Directive?"

I was running out of options and Tiger was running out of time. I had one move. If I miscalculated, Tiger was as good as dead—those blades would shred her where she lay.

I turned and threw my karambits at Tiger.

Being runically enhanced, they traveled faster than Regina's blades, reaching Tiger before hers. They crashed into the group of blades, disrupting their path. Both my blades managed to stop Regina's attack, but left me open, momentarily defenseless.

Exactly what Regina wanted.

"I *knew* you were weak," Regina said as she appeared next to me. A violet glow suffused her eyes, and I knew the amethyst was taking over, destroying her body and mind. She lunged forward and buried a blade in my midsection, ripping it across my abdomen in one smooth move. I looked down and Grey's words about samurai and seppuku raced to my memory. "You...chose...wrong."

She laughed as she gazed at me falling to my knees, bleeding on the grass. With a quick rotation of her body, she drove a leg into my chest and sent me flying. I landed on my back with brutal force and coughed up blood.

"I choose what I have always chosen," I managed, pulling her blade out of my body and releasing a healing cast on myself. It calmed the pain for the moment and let me think, but I knew it wouldn't be enough. I needed real help. I looked down at the blade I had removed. It was black—poisoned. I tossed the blade to the side, realizing my fate. "I choose the Directive. I will always choose the Directive."

"How dare you!" she screamed. "I will make you suffer the same way you made me suffer."

She slashed both arms across her body and formed a horde of glowing red blades which she held suspended and aimed at Tiger, who was still slumped at the base of the tree. I estimated no less than thirty to forty blades headed Tiger's way.

There was no way I could save Tiger if she released that horde of blades.

"These blades are special, love," Regina said sweetly. "I made them special for you and your Directive. I covered them in null runes. Tiger's shields won't stop those." She pointed at the cloud of death meant for Tiger. "They will punch through any defense and into her body. Did I forget to mention, they're poisoned too?"

I stared, coughed up some more blood and focused my

gaze on Tiger, who was defenseless and exposed. Tiger, who had wanted to save Regina if it was at all possible.

I had just killed her.

It was only a matter of time before death reached her and ripped her life from her. I felt the anger build low in my chest. I was not going to lose another member of the Directive—not tonight and not under my watch.

"I'm not the only one who has been poisoned," I said. "You need help. Let me help you. We need to get that gem out."

"You're pathetic," she spat, looking at me. "I am about to kill your second-in-command, and you want to help me? You weak, pathetic waste of space, how could I ever want to have you in my life? How could I think you were worthy of sharing my life? What was I thinking? You're a coward."

"You're not yourself," I said. "Let me help you."

"I'm going to do you one last favor, my love," she said. "I'm going to end your pitiful existence. Goodbye, Sebastian."

The timer on my watch went off.

Ten minutes had elapsed and the night exploded in power.

A group of thirty large figures covered in full armor appeared in Sheep Meadow in the next moment. I sensed a group of them form around Tiger and create a protective shield around her body. The rest of them raced into the Meadow and the night.

The horde of blades poised to destroy Tiger, dematerialized.

Grey who really wasn't Grey anymore, unleashed a low bone-curdling laugh, and rushed at Mura who realized too late that whatever he was fighting, wasn't an old, washed-up Night Warden. I saw Mura slash down only to see his arm sail away into the night.

"So soft and fragile," Grey said in his strange voice. "What challenge is this, Warden?" Grey turned and looked at Regina for a brief moment, before returning to Mura who had fallen to his knees. "Very well, I will leave the woman alone, but this one,"—Grey nodded his head at Mura—"this one is mine."

Grey stepped forward as his blade exploded in black energy and enveloped Mura.

Seconds later, the giant was gone and Grey fell forward.

"What have you done?" Regina demanded. "What are those?"

"I stopped you," I said, glancing at the large figures around Tiger. "You're not going to hurt the Directive or anyone else anymore."

"No..." she said, shaking her head as her voice trailed off. "You can't do this. I have the Sacred Amethyst, I have the power. You can't stop me, no one can stop me. Maledicta is mine. This city is mine. It belongs to me, it's rightfully mine...Mine!"

I knew I didn't have much time left. I could feel the poison burning through my body.

I unleashed the stasis darkcast and focused on Regina.

Black energy raced from my body and covered the ground around me, enveloping Regina. She screamed as the energy covered her completely. In moments, her screams were muffled and then completely silenced. She stood still, frozen in place.

I saw the stasis darkcast form around us both.

I felt the connection as the darkcast formed a siphon between us. I could feel her energy surge within her body. The Sacred Amethyst pulsed with power as the darkcast began draining it.

Violet energy blasted into the night sky, rising up from where she stood. It rose for several dozen feet and then descended back into her body with an explosion of light.

I looked down and saw black lines of energy had formed across my skin. Each one racing up my arms as the power from Regina traveled to me. The lines crisscrossed, forming a network that rapidly spread out across my entire body.

In seconds, I could feel the power of the darkcast building.

As I realized she was locked within the cast, pain wracked my body with a grip of steel. I focused my mind and finished the cast, feeling the link between us solidify and squeeze my chest tight.

I focused on Regina and saw her crumple to the ground. As she fell, I realized we were now racing against time.

"To me," I said to the nearest Rakshasa. It bowed low, then placed a fist on its chest. "Please take the injured to Ivory, but she"—I pointed to Regina—"has limited time. She needs to get to Ivory, right now. Do you know where she is?"

The Rakshasa looked down at me and nodded, gently scooping up Regina in its massive arms. The next moment, that Rakshasa, joined by two others, one carrying Grey, and the other carrying Tiger, raced off into the night.

I was feeling the effects of the darkcast and looked up into the night sky.

"This is a good night to die," I muttered as I felt the intensity of the poison increase in my body. "At least...at least the Directive is safe."

"Not time to die yet...charkin," a familiar voice said. "Take him to Ivory too. Tell her he's been poisoned. Here is the blade that struck him. She can use that to counter the poison."

I felt myself being lifted.

Out of the corner of my eye, I thought I saw an old woman dressed in white, walking out of the Park. It was only for a brief moment. When I tried to focus on her, she was gone and only the night remained.

I felt the Rakshasa turn and pick up speed as the stars in the night sky filled my vision.

THIRTY-ONE

"You should be dead," Ivory said as I sat up. "Fortunately for you, a stasis darkcast is a simple thing to undo."

"Simple?" I said wincing as I looked around. Ivory had converted one of the rooms in Tavern on the Green into a ward resembling those in her Tower. "What is this place? Where are we?"

"We are still in Sheep Meadow, Tavern on the Green," she said. "I merely took some liberties in order to provide adequate medical attention."

My body was still feeling the effects of the darkcast and the poison. My breathing was ragged and I was exhausted as I stumbled forward getting out of the bed.

"Be still," Ivory said, pointing a finger at me. "You will recover fully momentarily. You were poisoned—nasty stuff—and your body is worn out, exhausted from the darkcast. Give it a few moments more."

She was right. In about a minute, all the exhaustion left my body. The agony I was feeling earlier in my midsection disappeared slowly and I felt like myself again.

"That's...that's amazing," I said, looking around. "Regina?"

"I have her body in temporary stasis," she said. "I knew you would want to be present for this moment. You remember your vow—success or failure?"

"I do," I said, slowly moving my body and feeling energized. "I still hold true to my word."

"Good," she said. She waved at the Rakshasa who proceeded to step outside and guard the door. Tiger came in then, followed by a ragged-looking Grey. "Anyone else?"

I shook my head.

"No one else," I said. "Begin, please."

Ivory raised a hand and another white orb shot into the sky. It slowly descended and formed a white dome of energy over Tavern on the Green, cutting us off from everything.

"No disturbances now," Ivory said and headed into an adjacent room with the rest of us in tow. "This way. We still have time."

Regina was laying on a platform of soft white energy which rested on two reinforced tables in the center of the room.

"Is she—?"

"She lives, but has suffered much damage," Ivory answered, shaking her head. "Much damage. I will do what I can."

I nodded as Ivory placed her hands on Regina.

White light flowed from her fingers and transformed into a bloom of reds, oranges, blues, violets and greens. Ivory took the different strands of colors and wove them into one beam of intertwined colors. She grasped the multicolored beam and pressed it into Regina's chest.

Black energy slowly rose up the beam as she firmly held onto it. The amount of power filling the room was staggering. I remained by Ivory's side until the black energy traveling up the beam reached the top.

Once it did, Ivory extended a palm and removed the

entire beam of colors from Regina's chest. In her hand, it coalesced into a large amethyst filled with cracks.

Each of the cracks was bursting with black energy which whispered promises of untold power. All I had to do was take hold of the amethyst and I could—*thwack!*

Ivory had *thwacked* me across the face, bringing me to my senses. The allure of that gem's power was strong, and I stepped back, away from it. I could still sense it whispering to me, calling to me. I shook my head and stepped back even farther.

"Corruption is what this is," Ivory said, lifting up the amethyst. "Poison for someone like her"—she looked down at Regina—"you too. Poison that should be destroyed. What say you, Warden?"

She held out the amethyst to Grey who shook his head.

"I have enough nastiness inside to deal with," he said. "I don't need anymore. Destroy that thing, we'll be better off with it gone."

"Very good," Ivory said with a satisfied nod. "There is still much light in you. Stronger than the darkness."

"You could have just asked," he said gruffly. "No need to test me."

"The test was needed," Ivory said. "Much darkness is on the horizon. I needed to make sure."

"Make sure of what?"

"Make sure the Night Warden is ready for the coming darkness," she said, taking the amethyst in her other hand and holding it up to the light. "Wordweavers have much to answer for. This is an abomination."

She closed her hand and squeezed.

White light suffused her closed fist, and the amethyst disintegrated into a fine, white powder.

"Will she be—?" I started. "How much damage?"

Ivory placed a finger on Regina's forehead and then slowly

walked outside, leaving me alone in the room with Regina and no answer. Grey and Tiger slowly followed her out, giving us some privacy.

Regina opened her eyes and sat up. For a brief moment, what seemed to be a flicker of recognition flashed in her eyes and faded from view.

She looked at me with a puzzled expression and slowly scanned the room. After she took in the room, she returned her perplexed gaze back to my face as if trying to find something familiar.

"Do I know you?" she asked. "Part of me feels like we know each other. You feel familiar to me, but I just can't place your face. Do we know each other?"

Ivory had stepped back into the room and stood silently by my side. She placed a hand on my forearm and looked at Regina.

"No," I said. "We found you in the Park not too long ago. It seems you suffered a head injury and may be suffering some loss of memory. Do you remember your name, or where you live?"

"My name is Regina...Regina Clark and I live downtown in Soho," she said. "I seem to remember some things, but other things are a blur."

I nodded.

Realization dawned on me that she recalled her life with the exception of anything that pertained to me.

"Do you know this man?" Ivory asked as if to drive the point home. "Does he look familiar at all?"

Regina stared at my face intently. After what felt like an hour, but was closer to thirty seconds, she shook her head.

"I'm sorry, no," she said finally. "Should he be familiar?"

"No," I said. "I'm glad you're okay. The Park can be dangerous at night."

Grey walked in and nodded in my direction.

"I have an EMTe headed our way," he said. "Roxanne will admit her into Haven and run some tests to make sure there's no other lasting damage."

"Thank you," I said, my voice failing me. "I appreciate it."

"You ever need to talk, you know where to find me," Grey said and shook my hand. "I'll swing by the Church soon."

I nodded silently as he placed a hand on my shoulder and left the room. Ivory began speaking with Regina, reforming her memories as they conversed about Regina's life.

Tiger came in and stayed close to my side.

A few minutes later, Ivory stepped out, following Grey. I heard the EMTe pull up. Regina made to leave, pausing at the door and turning.

"I was told you were the one who found me," she said, looking at me. "Thank you for bringing me to safety. I don't know how I can ever repay you."

"No need to repay me, really," I said. "Be safe and live a good life. That would be payment enough."

"Are you certain?"

"Absolutely," I said. "Live your best life—Regina, is it?"

She nodded.

"Yes, thank you again," she said. "I better get going."

"I understand," I said. "You will always be welcome."

She gave me a strange look, twisted my heart with a smile, and stepped out the door and out of my life.

Tiger sighed and shook her head.

"It's for the best, Seb."

"I know," I said. "Doesn't mean I have to like it."

"No, no it doesn't, but at least she's alive, the amethyst has been destroyed, you still have the Directive, and the Directive still has you," she said. "You still have your family. We'll always be here for you."

"Thank you," I said. "Can I have a few moments?"

"Of course," she said. "Want to meet back at the Church?"

"Yes," I said. "I'll make my way back, just need some time to think...you know, clear my head."

She nodded and left the room. Leaving me alone with my thoughts and the specters of my past.

I exited the main building and stepped into the night—alone.

THIRTY-TWO

Or so I thought.

I was heading out of the Park when I sensed her.

"How long have you been following me?"

"Since you left Tavern on the Green," she said, materializing beside me. "That was quite the fight. I was impressed. Now I know why Char picked you two."

"I didn't know dragons could become invisible."

"There's plenty about us most don't know," Cynder said. "Invisibility is child's play. It's just the manipulation of light."

"True," I said with a nod. "Mura is gone, what of Maledicta?"

"Alexander, despite his protests, is acting on that now," she said. "He's using our vast resources to locate and reintegrate the survivors. Maledicta will cease to exist in name only. The members of the group will now be folded into our organization."

"It's the most logical step," I said, stepping out of the Park onto Central Park West and 59th Street. "You goaded her into attacking us."

"Yes, I did," she said. "You needed her desperate and unstable, well, the unstable part was done by the amethyst. I merely gave her some incentive."

"You never left the Meadow."

"No, I didn't," she answered, looking across the street. "The Rakshasa were an unexpected and inspired twist. Kudos on utilizing them to even the playing field."

"Thank you," I said, looking at her warily. "You're here to congratulate me?"

"I'm here to inform you of some news."

"News?"

"I wanted you to hear it from me first," she said. "Once cleared by Haven, Regina will be relocated overseas. She will be cared for financially and assigned a security detail."

"Not that I'm unappreciative, but why?" I asked. "She's not one of your Wyvern."

"Not my call," she said. "You want detailed answers, go ask Char. Good luck getting them."

"I see," I said. "I'll have to thank her in person then."

"You do that," she said. "If you want my opinion, she wants you to have clarity of purpose and unwavering focus."

"She feels Regina would be a distraction?"

"You disagree?"

I paused for a few moments before answering.

"No," I said. "Maybe not now or soon, but eventually she would be."

"Char has plans for her charkin," she said, turning and walking away. "Clarity of purpose and unwavering focus. There's a war brewing. You and your Directive need to be ready. Goodnight, little brother."

I turned to answer her, but she was gone.

I headed home to the Church and my family.

If there was a war brewing, we were going to fight it on

our terms. The dragons may be fearsome, but no one crosses the Stray Dogs and continues to draw breath.

No one.

THE END

AUTHOR NOTES

Thank you for reading this story and jumping into the world of Treadwell Supernatural Directive with me.

Disclaimer: The Author Notes are written at the very end of the writing process. This section is not seen by the ART or my amazing Jeditor. Any typos or errors following this disclaimer are mine and mine alone.

I spent some time alone with Sebastian.

The family you create is, at times, more important than the family you are born into. This story was a bit more raw for him than the others. His smooth unflappable exterior wasn't as present in this story, because it dealt with someone he cared about. Someone he loved.

Regina.

In many parts of this story he was unsure, off-balance and awkward. Unlike Tiger, who seemed to have it all together most of the time.

That was intentional.

Think back to your first serious partner. How did you

feel? Butterflies in the stomach? Anxious? Brain slightly malfunctioning most of the time? Now amplify that feeling 10x.

That's where Sebastian is when it comes to Regina—except in one area.

The Directive.

Those feelings don't impact how Sebastian feels about the Directive. There he has complete clarity. He knows where he stands and more importantly, where *they* stand in his life. There is no question, that for Sebastian, the Directive comes first.

It's not a matter of right or wrong.

He doesn't view it through that lens. For him its a matter of the Directive being his created family. He will do what it takes to keep them safe and to see them grow.

Nothing else really matters for him.

Some may call that obsessed and others will see it as driven to do his duty. The Directive is his duty and nothing and no one can change that.

It's why he makes the choices he makes, and why he accepts the outcome. He understands that if he can't have what he desires, the woman he loves, in his life, then at the very least she will be safe and secure wherever she is. (unless of course she has a relapse and the part of her mind where Sebastian lives, resurfaces...hmmmm).

That being said, there's a war coming.

This isn't the last you will see of The Stray Dogs, there are many other stories where they can visit, but for now, this book will pause their specific stories.

I look forward to seeing where they will pop up. They still have to pay Dex a visit at the Montague School of Battle Magic, we still don't know what exactly is Ivory's agenda, and there is a certain cranky Night Warden who may need an assist from them in the future.

We will definitely see them again soon.

I really enjoyed writing ENDGAME TANGO.

The world of Sebastian, Tiger & Co. is a darker and grittier world which has a different nuance than M&S. For me as an author, writing MS&P is like coming home. Comfortable and familiar. The words flow almost of their own will.

Every time you give me the space to step outside of that world a bit, even if it's to visit another part of the same world, I learn more about myself as a creative and author. For this I humbly and profoundly thank you for being my amazing reader.

You encourage me and give me (not-so-subtle) hints about what may or may not be working. I wanted to express my deepest apologies for a lack of ART on this one. I know there is a hardcore group of SHREDDERS (*snikt!*) who look forward to the ART phase of the stories.

I promise to make it up to you on the next story—IMMORTAL M&S 23.

Polish those claws!

The ART wasn't present for this story due to marketing conflicts and my desire to get the story out to you. That one falls on my shoulders, so I'll take the heat for any typos or continuity issues and will kindly accept any corrections you point out to me post-publication.

If you didn't know, I have the most outstanding, incredible, generous, witty, and funny readers on the planet, and I feel your support every time I publish a book.

You truly all totally rock! (I read that and realize how dated I sound lol! But it's true!)

(time for the profound, but non-negotiable part of the author notes)

If you gotten this far—thank you.

I appreciate you as a reader and a daring adventurer, jumping into these imaginings of my mind, and joining me as we step into these incredible stories and worlds.

You are amazing!

Thank you again for jumping into this story with me!

SUPPORT US

Patreon
The Magick Squad

Website/Newsletter
www.orlandoasanchez.com

JOIN US

Facebook
Montague & Strong Case Files

Youtube
Bitten Peaches Publishing Storyteller

Instagram
bittenpeaches

Email
orlando@orlandoasanchez.com

M&S World Store
Emandes

BITTEN PEACHES PUBLISHING

Thanks for Reading!
If you enjoyed this book, would you please **leave a review** at the site you purchased it from? It doesn't have to be long... just a line or two would be fantastic and it would really help me out.

Bitten Peaches Publishing offers more books and audiobooks
across various genres including: urban fantasy, science fiction, adventure, & mystery!

www.BittenPeachesPublishing.com

More books by Orlando A. Sanchez

Montague & Strong Detective Agency Novels
Tombyards & Butterflies•Full Moon Howl•Blood is Thicker•Silver Clouds Dirty Sky•Homecoming•Dragons & Demigods•Bullets & Blades•Hell Hath No Fury•Reaping Wind•The Golem•Dark Glass•Walking the

Razor•Requiem•Divine Intervention•Storm Blood•Revenant•Blood Lessons•Broken Magic•Lost Runes•Archmage•Entropy•Corpse Road

Montague & Strong Detective Agency Stories
No God is Safe•The Date•The War Mage•A Proper Hellhound•The Perfect Cup•Saving Mr. K

Night Warden Novels
Wander•ShadowStrut•Nocturne Melody

Rule of the Council
Blood Ascension•Blood Betrayal•Blood Rule

The Warriors of the Way
The Karashihan•The Spiritual Warriors•The Ascendants•The Fallen Warrior•The Warrior Ascendant•The Master Warrior

John Kane
The Deepest Cut•Blur

Sepia Blue
The Last Dance•Rise of the Night•Sisters•Nightmare•Nameless•Demon

Chronicles of the Modern Mystics
The Dark Flame•A Dream of Ashes

The Treadwell Supernatural Directive
The Stray Dogs•Shadow Queen•Endgame Tango

Brew & Chew Adventures
Hellhound Blues

Bangers & Mash
Bangers & Mash

Tales of the Gatekeepers
Bullet Ballet•The Way of Bug•Blood Bond

Division 13
The Operative•The Magekiller

Blackjack Chronicles
The Dread Warlock

The Assassin's Apprentice
The Birth of Death

Gideon Shepherd Thrillers
Sheepdog

DAMNED
Aftermath

Nyxia White
They Bite•They Rend•They Kill

Iker the Cleaner
Iker the Unseen•Daystrider•Nightwalker

Stay up to date with new releases!
Shop www.orlandoasanchez.com for more books and audiobooks!

ART SHREDDERS

I want to take a moment to extend a special thanks to the ART SHREDDERS.

No book is the work of one person. I am fortunate enough to have an amazing team of advance readers and shredders.

Thank you for giving of your time and keen eyes to provide notes, insights, answers to the questions, and corrections (dealing wonderfully with my extreme dreaded comma allergy). You help make every book and story go from good to great. Each and every one of you helped make this book fantastic, and I couldn't do this without each of you.

THANK YOU

PATREON SUPPORTERS

Exclusive short stories
Premium Access to works in progress
Free Ebooks for select tiers

Join here
The Magick Squad

THANK YOU

Alisha Harper, Amber Dawn Sessler, Angela Tapping, Anne Morando, Anthony Hudson, Ashley Britt

Brenda French

Carolyn J. Evans, Carrie O'Leary, Cindy Deporter, Connie Cleary

Dan Bergemann, Dan Fong, David Smith, Davis Johnson, Diane Garcia, Diane Jackson, Diane Kassmann, Dorothy Phillips

Elizabeth Varga, Enid Rodriguez, Eric Maldonato, Eve Bartlet, Ewan Mollison

Federica De Dominicis, Fluff Chick Productions,

Gail Ketcham Hermann, Gary McVicar, Groove72

Ingrid Schijven

James Burns, James Wheat, Jasmine Breeden, Jasmine Davis, Jeffrey Juchau, Jo Dungey, Joe Durham, John Fauver (in memoriam), Joy Kiili, Just Jeanette

Kathy Ringo, Krista Fox

Leona Jackson, Lisa Simpson, Lizzette Piltch

Malcolm Robertson, Mark Morgan, Mark Price, MaryAnn Sims,

Mary Barzee, Mary Beth Wright, Maureen McCallan, Mel Brown, Melissa Miller, Meri, Duncanson

Paige Guido, Patricia Pearson, Peter Griffin

Ralph Kroll, Renee Penn, Robert Walters

Sara M Branson, Sara N Morgan, Sarah Sofianos, Sassy Bear, Sharon Elliott, Shelby, Sonyia Roy, Stacey Stein, Steven Huber, Susan Bowin, Susan Spry

Tami Cowles, Terri Adkisson, Tommy, Trish Brown

Van Nebedum

Wanda Corder-Jones, Wendy Schindler, WS Dawkins

***

I want to extend a special note of gratitude to all of our
Patrons in
The Magick Squad.

Your generous support helps me to continue on this amazing
adventure called 'being an author'.
I deeply and truly appreciate each of you for your selfless act
of patronage.

You are all amazing beyond belief.

THANK YOU

ACKNOWLEDGEMENTS

With each book, I realize that every time I learn something about this craft, it highlights so many things I still have to learn. Each book, each creative expression, has a large group of people behind it.

This book is no different.

Even though you see one name on the cover, it is with the knowledge that I am standing on the shoulders of the literary giants that informed my youth, and am supported by my generous readers who give of their time to jump into the adventures of my overactive imagination.

I would like to take a moment to express my most sincere thanks:

To Dolly: My wife and greatest support. You make all this possible each and every day. You keep me grounded when I get lost in the forest of ideas. Thank you for asking the right questions when needed, and listening intently when I go off on tangents. Thank you for who you are and the space you create—I love you.

To my Tribe: You are the reason I have stories to tell. You cannot possibly fathom how much and how deeply I love you all.

To Lee: Because you were the first audience I ever had. I love you, sis.

To the Logsdon Family: The words *thank you* are insufficient to describe the gratitude in my heart for each of you. JL, your support always demands I bring my best, my A-game, and produce the best story I can. Both you and Lorelei (my Uber Jeditor) and now, Audrey, are the reason I am where I am today. My thank you for the notes, challenges, corrections, advice, and laughter. Your patience is truly infinite. *Arigatogozaimasu.*

To The Montague & Strong Case Files Group—AKA The MoB (Mages of Badassery): When I wrote T&B there were fifty-five members in The MoB. As of this release, there are over one thousand five hundred members in the MoB. I am honored to be able to call you my MoB Family. Thank you for being part of this group and M&S.

You make this possible. **THANK YOU.**

To the ever-vigilant PACK: You help make the MoB...the MoB. Keeping it a safe place for us to share and just...be. Thank you for your selfless vigilance. You truly are the Sentries of Sanity.

Chris Christman II: A real-life technomancer who makes the **MoBTV LIVEvents +Kaffeeklatsch** on YouTube amazing. Thank you for your tireless work and wisdom. Everything is connected...you totally rock!

To the WTA—The Incorrigibles: JL, Ben Z., Eric QK., S.S., and Noah.

They sound like a bunch of badass misfits, because they are. My exposure to the deranged and deviant brain trust you all represent helped me be the author I am today. I have officially gone to the *dark side* thanks to all of you. I humbly give you my thanks, and...it's all your fault.

To my fellow Indie Authors: I want to thank each of you for creating a space where authors can feel listened to, and encouraged to continue on this path. A rising tide lifts all the ships indeed.

To The English Advisory: Aaron, Penny, Carrie, Davina, and all of the UK MoB. For all things English...thank you.

To DEATH WISH COFFEE: This book (and every book I write) has been fueled by generous amounts of the only coffee on the planet (and in space) strong enough to power my very twisted imagination. Is there any other coffee that can compare? I think not. DEATH WISH—thank you!

To Deranged Doctor Design: Kim, Darja, Tanja, Jovana, and Milo (Designer Extraordinaire).

If you've seen the covers of my books and been amazed, you can thank the very talented and gifted creative team at DDD. They take the rough ideas I give them, and produce incredible covers that continue to surprise and amaze me. Each time, I find myself striving to write a story worthy of the covers they produce. DDD, you embody professionalism and creativity. Thank you for the great service and spectacular covers. **YOU GUYS RULE!**

To you, the reader: I was always taught to save the best for last. I write these stories for **you**. Thank you for jumping down the rabbit holes of ***what if?*** with me. You are the reason I write the stories I do.

You keep reading...I'll keep writing.

Thank you for your support and encouragement.

SPECIAL MENTIONS

To Dolly: my rock, anchor, and inspiration. Thank you...always.

Larry & Tammy—The WOUF: Because even when you aren't there...you're there.

Orlando A. Sanchez
www.orlandoasanchez.com

Orlando has been writing ever since his teens when he was immersed in creating scenarios for playing Dungeons and Dragons with his friends every weekend.

The worlds of his books are urban settings with a twist of the paranormal lurking just behind the scenes and with generous doses of magic, martial arts, and mayhem.

He currently resides in Queens, NY with his wife and children.

Thanks for Reading!

If you enjoyed this book
Please leave a review & share!
(with everyone you know)

It would really help us out!

Printed in Great Britain
by Amazon